FINDING HOME

GARRETT LEIGH

Cover Art: Garrett Leigh @ Black Jazz Design

Photography: Dan Burgess @ Dan Burgess Photography/Vagabond Shooter

Original Edits: Carole-Ann Galloway & Alex Whitehall

Additional Proofing: Jay Northcote

For Darcey

PROLOGUE

The old Swindon house had broken doors. They stuck, never closed properly, or opened on the first try. The front door was no exception. Until the fateful morning Dennis Hendry kicked it open with a single blow of his steel-capped boot.

"Wendy! Where are you?"

Leo jumped and jostled Lila, who was eating her Shreddies beside him. Milk sloshed onto the table, and their mother froze, dishcloth in hand. "Oh God. It's your dad. Leo, quick! Get in the cupboard."

The front door banged again as Dennis slammed it shut. Leo gathered Lila in his arms and scrambled for the cupboard under the stairs—the dark, cramped place where they'd hidden from Dennis and his rage for as long as Leo could remember.

A shadow darkened the kitchen doorway as they made it inside. Wendy moved to block the cupboard door and nudged it shut with her foot. Inky blackness swallowed them, save for a crack of light just wide enough for Leo to see his father's face for the first time in six months.

Bastard. Weathered, and flushed with booze and rage, Dennis hadn't changed. He slammed his fist on the kitchen table, and more milk spilled out of Lila's bowl. "Look at this bloody mess. This how you keep my house, eh?"

"It's only milk," Wendy said. "What are you doing here?"

"What do you think?"

Dennis towered over Wendy, leering with his flinty gaze. She leaned back, and he caught her by the throat. "Oh, no, you don't. You stay put and hear how it's going to be. I'm getting tired of that manky bedsit. I want to sort this nonsense out today."

"Dennis—"

Wendy's plea was cut off by the squeeze of Dennis's hand around her neck. He tightened his grip until her face reddened and her eyes bulged. Then he let her go with a sneer. "Clean this mess up, then sit down. We're going to have a little talk."

Wendy didn't argue. She shot a furtive glance Leo's way, and set about clearing the detritus of their abandoned breakfast: Lila's Shreddies, Leo's toast. She picked up her own teacup, and her hand began to shake.

Dennis growled. "Get on with it, woman."

Woman. A sudden coldness swept over Leo, and the panic in his heart subsided to a steady beat of fear-laced rage. He closed his eyes and imagined bursting out of the cupboard and punching Dennis so hard his teeth shattered, like the plates Dennis threw against the wall when his whisky ran out. Or grabbing the cricket bat leaning against the door and cracking him over the head with it.

Instead, he opened his eyes and remembered the instructions left by the kindly policeman who'd accompanied them to court to file the restraining order: *"Don't fight him. Call for help."*

Leo reached behind him. His mother's handbag hung open on the hook, like it always did. He felt around and found her phone, swiping at it until the screen flashed to life. *Shit.* Leo flinched and eyed the gap in the door, but Wendy had Dennis's attention.

She set the breadboard on the side as he watched her every move. "You're not supposed to be here."

Dennis folded his arms across his broad chest. "Do you think I was stupid enough to listen to them coppers, you daft bitch?"

"What do you *want*, Dennis?"

"I want what's mine. I got the papers in the post this morning. Divorce, eh? Who the fuck do you think you are?"

Wendy sighed. "We've been separated for long enough now. Please, Dennis. You need to *go*."

"It's my bloody house! My house, my things, my kids."

Dennis took a menacing step forward. Leo instinctively tightened his grip on Lila.

"The kids aren't here," Wendy said, her voice rising in pitch. "Take what you want and leave."

"Not here, eh?" Dennis glanced up at the ceiling. "Maybe I should go and check. Is Leo in bed? Maybe I should drag him out by his poofy hair. Show him my belt again."

It was Dennis's favourite way to break Wendy, certain in the knowledge that she'd do anything—take anything—to protect her children. But this time, she didn't falter. "Check all you want, then get the hell out."

Dennis turned his lips up in a snarl, and his impotent posturing morphed into deadly fury. He lunged for Wendy and grabbed her hair. Her terrified shriek rang out as Leo jammed 999 into the phone.

"Emergency services operator. Which service do you require?"

"My dad's hurting my mum."

"Speak up," the operator said. "I can't hear you. Can you tell me your name?"

Dennis threw Wendy against the wall. The impact rattled her bones and snapped her head back.

"Please," Leo whispered.

Dennis seized the abandoned bread knife from the kitchen counter. Leo closed his eyes. Buried his face in Lila's sweet-scented hair. A dull thud rattled his skull, then another, and another, like the kicks and punches he'd heard so many times before.

But this wasn't like the other times. Wendy's gasp was different, stuttered and strangled. Empty. Hopeless. The phone line buzzed and crackled. Leo counted three heartbeats before the operator took a breath.

"Hello? Are you still on the line? Which service do you require? Do you need assistance?"

Leo opened his eyes. Blood oozed across the tiled kitchen floor.

Wendy's blood.

Mum's blood.

Dennis was by the stove, bending down with an unlit cigarette in his mouth. A nearby tea towel caught alight. He shoved it aside into the stack of newspapers ready for recycling. They ignited. Leo watched the flames begin their dance, and clutched the phone tighter. "Come quickly. My dad just killed my mum and set the house on fire."

ONE

Charlie de Sousa made himself comfortable on the bottom of the stairs. The third step up was the best one. The bottom two creaked like crazy, and though he wouldn't get in real trouble for eavesdropping on his parents, he didn't want to interrupt their discussion before they got to the juicy bit.

"It's a risk, Kate," Reg said. Charlie could almost see him running his hands through his unruly mop of white hair. "Taking one traumatised child is a challenge in itself, but two? I don't know. Do we even have room?"

"Of course we have room." Charlie heard Kate get up and pace around, like she always did when she was annoyed. "The boy can go in the study. We'll just have to move the computer downstairs."

"It's not ideal."

"'Ideal'? For God's sake, Reg. Nothing ever is. If it was, these kids wouldn't need us in the first place."

Silence. Charlie strained his ears and wondered if the conversation was continuing in sign language. Kate was hard of hearing, and could read lips and speak, but she and Reg often continued conversations in sign language if they didn't want the rest of the house to eavesdrop. Charlie considered creeping to the door and taking a peek, but Reg *always* caught him when he did that. The bloke had ninja senses.

Someone in the dining room sighed; Charlie couldn't tell who. Then Kate spoke again. "Look, I know it's a big ask, but these kids have been through the mill. They need a safe place to heal, and we can give them that. I *know* we can."

"What about the family we already have?" Reg countered. "It says here that both kids have medical issues from that fire, and the boy was in trouble at school before that . . . fighting and drinking. Truancy. Is it really fair to bring that into our home?"

"We can help them," Kate said. "And we should ask the others before we make a decision. It's how we do things in this house."

Reg's dry laugh told Charlie that Kate had got her way. He tensed, ready to flee upstairs, but the dining room door opened before he could move. Reg fixed him with a stare that said he'd known Charlie was there all along. "Go fetch your sister. I'm going to call Andy. Family meeting as soon as we're all here."

Charlie scrambled upstairs. He found Fliss in her room, headphones on, watching some vampire crap while she talked to her mates on Facebook. She didn't acknowledge him, even when he blocked her view, but that wasn't unusual. Charlie had joined the Poulton family when he'd been barely two. Fliss had been six, and the only child in Reg and Kate's full time care back then. She'd never quite forgiven Charlie for encroaching on her territory, and that suited Charlie fine. Fliss was a stuck-up bitch, and she *always* used all the hot water.

He unplugged her headphones.

She hissed and punched his arm. "What the hell are you doing?"

"Dad wants us. Family meeting."

"What for?"

Charlie shrugged. He wasn't about to share his stolen knowledge with Fliss. Stuff that. He'd enjoy her being the last to know. "Just come downstairs, yeah?"

He left without waiting for her response. Kate would deal with Fliss if she didn't show.

Charlie drifted downstairs and took his place at the dining room table. Kate appeared and set a big bowl of her special houmous in the middle of the table, a sure sign that the discussion might get heavy. In this house, nothing soothed frayed nerves better than Kate's home cooking.

She ruffled Charlie's hair. "Okay, chicken?"

Charlie scowled and fixed his too-long dark hair, but he didn't mean it. He enjoyed Kate's motherly affection far more than he cared to let on. "Did Dad get hold of Andy?"

"He's on his way. Have you done your homework?"

Charlie waited until Kate had finished faffing with the table, then quickly translated what he wanted to say into signs that would make sense—or, at least, quickly for him. Kate switched between signing and English like breathing. For Charlie, it took a little more thought. *"Yes. Just art left. Dad will help me."*

Kate smiled and flitted in and out of the room a dozen more times until Charlie's burly older brother arrived a little while later.

Andy Poulton filled the room and lifted Kate off her feet in a bruising bear hug. "All right, Ma?"

Kate beamed. Andy was Reg's son from his first marriage, but he'd called Kate *Ma* since she'd married Reg twenty years ago, and there wasn't much that made her happier. "How's the cat?"

Andy grimaced. "She shredded the couch again."

"Maybe you should get another one to keep her company? She's probably bored while you're at work all day."

"Nah. I think she's evil."

"I don't believe that, sweetheart. She just needs some love."

Andy grunted and swiped a finger through the houmous. "Anyway, why am I here? Dad said it was important. Is something wrong?"

Kate glanced briefly at Charlie and shook her head. "No, no. It's nothing like that. Let's wait for the others, then your dad and I will explain everything."

She left the room to fetch drinks. Andy dropped into the chair beside him and ruffled Charlie's hair.

"Stop it," Charlie snapped. What was it with people messing with his bloody hair?

Andy chuckled. "Got a girlfriend yet?"

"Piss off."

"What? Not even a snog up the cricket pavilion?"

"Piss *off*." Charlie cringed and angled himself away from Andy. Was it too much to ask that his own brother didn't pester him too?

Apparently oblivious, Andy laughed again and put a fraternal arm around Charlie's shoulders. "Easy, mate. Just pulling your leg. Where's Fliss?"

"Upstairs."

"Did you tell her about the meeting?"

Charlie turned to Reg as he entered the room. "I tried."

Reg gave him a patient glance and banged on the ceiling. "Fliss! Downstairs. Now."

It took a while for them all to settle at the table. Beside Andy, Charlie waited for Reg and Kate to drop their bomb.

Reg went first. "We got a call from social services this morning. Though we haven't taken any new children for a while, we're still, technically, available for emergency foster placements."

Here it comes.

Kate took over. "We've been asked to take two siblings, a boy and a girl, with immediate effect."

"No way." Fliss groaned. "I don't want the house full of screaming kids again. We've only just got rid of the last one."

"Freddie left more than a year ago," Reg said in the tone he reserved for Fliss when she got bratty. "And they aren't screaming kids. The boy is fifteen, the same as Charlie, and his sister is profoundly deaf."

"Is that why they want you to take them?" Andy asked. "So Ma can help with sign language and stuff?"

"Partly." Reg exchanged a look with Kate. "But there's a little more to it than that. They lost their mother a while ago in quite horrific circumstances, and they've both had some trouble, uh, settling since."

Reg's waver didn't go unnoticed. Fliss sat back in her chair and folded her arms. "Settling how? Are they nutters, or what? I'm not living with a pair of skanky ASBO kids."

"Fliss." Kate's tone was sharp. "That's not how we talk about people in this house. Mind your words and think before you speak."

Fliss rolled her eyes, but a stern frown from Kate cut off her inevitably spiky retort.

"What happened to their mum?" Charlie asked.

Reg shook his head. "I can't tell you that. If they do come to us, it'll be up to them if they want to share their story. For now, all we can tell you is that these kids very much need a home, and your mother and I would like to offer them one."

Offer. Charlie absorbed the word and turned the prospect over in his head. What if the kids didn't want to come? Reg and Kate were the best parents in the world, but the kids wouldn't know that.

"Where would they sleep?" Andy reached for the snacks Kate had spread on the table. "You've only got one spare room."

"And it's all set up and ready to go," Kate said. "The girl would sleep in there."

Of course she would. The room closest to Reg and Kate's had always been reserved for the newest kids, or the youngest, depending who needed them most.

"What about the boy?"

Charlie waited for Kate to repeat the proposition he'd over-heard her put to Reg. For all this was a family discussion, it seemed they had the finer details worked out already.

"We were thinking he could go in the study."

"The study?" Andy raised a doubtful eyebrow. "Bit small, isn't it?"

"Well, yes, but Charlie is just across the hall. We were thinking the boy could store most of his things in there."

Charlie sat up sharply. That wasn't the plan he'd overheard, and his cupboards were jam-packed with his own stuff. "You want him to share my space?"

"To start with," Kate said. "We'll get it sorted as soon as we can, but the interaction with you might do him some good."

"Interaction?"

"Contact. Conversation. These kids have been through a lot, and their files say neither of them sleep well. Having Andy around helped you settle when you first came to us."

Kate looked beseechingly at Andy, who took his cue. "It's true. You screamed the place down the first night we had you, then I came to stay for the summer holidays and voila: sleeping like a baby."

"I don't remember that."

Andy shrugged. "Why would you? It was just a few weeks, but it worked. Might help this kid too."

Reg nodded his agreement. "It would be temporary, Char-lie. We'd get some new furniture in due course."

"Okay . . ." Charlie was coming around to the idea. He'd

shared his wardrobe before. He could do it again, right? And perhaps a good clear out would do him good. "I'm in. I vote yes."

Fliss huffed. "So it's settled, then, is it? Charlie gets to decide for everyone?"

"Nothing's decided." Kate put her hand on the files Reg had brought to the table. "This is a big decision, and it affects us all. We'd like to help these children, but not at the expense of the family we already have. So please, keep asking your questions, and we'll do our best to answer them."

Charlie considered the offer. "Where are they now? With another family?"

"Yes, but no one there can sign for the little girl except the brother." Again, Kate looked to Reg. "They're in Swindon at the moment. Social services think they'd be better off starting out somewhere new."

"'Starting out'?" Fliss frowned again. "How long are they going to be here?"

"If . . ." Reg held up a hand to quiet Fliss. "*If* they come to us, how long they stay would depend on what we could do for them, and that hangs a little on the rest of you. Kate and I can't do this alone, and we wouldn't want to. We want to do this together, as a family."

Reg had a way with Fliss no one else did. After a protracted stare down, she relaxed—the aggression seeping out of her—and shrugged. "Whatever. Just keep them out of my room, yeah?"

"What are their names?" Andy asked.

"Leo and Lila. It says here that Lila likes arts and crafts and animals, and Leo . . ." Kate flipped through the thick file. "He likes football."

Leo: three tiny letters that changed the mysterious boy from an abstraction to a tangible person, in Charlie's mind at least.

"Football?" Fliss snorted. "He'll have fun with all Charlie's anime shit, then."

Charlie bristled, but a frown from Kate kept him quiet. He was no mug, but bitching with Fliss was a battle he'd surely lose. Who cared if she didn't know the difference between anime and manga?

Kate closed the file again. "Any more questions?"

Charlie couldn't think of any. He tuned out Andy's practical suggestions about building an extra cupboard. They'd put the decision about taking these kids to a vote, of course, but with Fliss on board, there was little need. It was happening, and Charlie refocussed on the discussion just in time to find out he'd have new housemates by the end of the week.

Later that night, Kate tapped on Charlie's open bedroom door. Charlie nodded, knowing she'd come in anyway, like she did most nights on her way to bed.

"How are you doing, sweetheart?"

Charlie tucked his drawing pad and pen under his pillow. "Okay."

"Okay?" Kate smiled. "Come on. You can do better than that, sunshine. We dropped a bomb on you today. Anything you want to talk about?"

"Nope."

"Nothing at all?"

"Nope."

"I brought you something." Kate took up her customary perch on the edge of Charlie's bed and held out an envelope. "Take a look."

Curious, Charlie opened it. Inside were two photographs: one of an angelic little girl and the other of a striking boy. The boy, tall and lean, with wild curly hair and sharp green eyes, was beautiful. Charlie compared the image with that of his sister.

Though they had different hair, their fair complexions gave them away as siblings.

That, and they both looked utterly miserable. "Is this them? Leo and Lila?"

"Yes, these were taken at Christmas in their last foster home."

Charlie thought back to the rowdy Poulton family Christmas just passed: Food, presents, laughter. "They don't seem very happy."

"I don't think they are, darling."

"Is that why you want them to come here so much?"

Kate smiled. "Reg knew you were sitting on the stairs."

That didn't surprise Charlie. Reg knew everything, even when he said nothing at all. "Is Leo going to come to school with me?"

"I hope so."

Kate's tone made Charlie look up from the photos. "You hope so? Why wouldn't he? I thought you said he was my age. Is he going to go to college or something instead?"

Kate held up her hand. "Slow down. Even after a decade of practice, I still can't lip-read in the dark."

"Sorry."

"That's okay. Repeat yourself, and I'll do my best to answer."

Charlie voiced his questions again with more consideration. Kate absorbed them with a nod. "Leo had a bit of trouble at his last school. We think it would be better if he settled in for a few days before we threw him into Heyton High."

"Trouble? What kind of trouble?"

Kate paused, clearly weighing up how much she could tell say without betraying the boy's confidence. "There have been a few incidents . . . fighting, and such. Nothing too out of the ordinary for boys your age, but that's part of the reason I—we—

would like him to spend some time with you. You're a good balm for a quick temper, chicken. I should know."

Charlie frowned. Kate often said cryptic things like that, and he never quite understood them.

She touched his cheek. "Don't think so hard, sweetheart. You've always been my little brooder."

"'Brooder'? Why are you so obsessed with poultry references?"

"Because I'm a mother hen." Kate grinned, but her gaze sobered as she rose to leave. "You've always been a calming influence on me, Charlie, in the same way Fliss's sharp tongue is good for your father's reticence. You remind us how human we are, and how much value there is in being different. Life would be boring if we were all the same."

It was a nice sentiment, but Charlie didn't see how it would help Leo stay out of fights at school. Heyton High was a pit of hormones, angst, and egos, and despite Kate's faith in him, not a day went by that Charlie didn't want to deck someone.

Not that there's anyone there worth decking.

Kate paused at the door, her hand on the handle. "Fliss thought you could stick some of those posters you did for the Olympics in Leo's room."

"She did?"

"Yes, she did. You know she's not as heartless as she makes herself out to be."

"If you say so." Charlie would have to take Kate's word for it, though a lifetime of living with Fliss told him that she was indeed a class-A bitch. "I'm not sure about the posters. The Olympics were years ago now. Do you really think he'll like them?"

"Can't hurt," Kate said. "I know they're not football, but he might like other sports too."

She said good night and left Charlie to it. Alone again, he

considered what artwork he could bear to part with, even if it was only going across the hall. The study was tiny, but if they put Leo's bed under the window, the posters could go on the ceiling.

Charlie closed his eyes, picturing the finished result, and fell asleep still holding the haunting photograph of the most beautiful boy he'd ever laid eyes on.

TWO

Heyton High School was the bane of Charlie's life, and never more so than at lunchtime. He didn't smoke, play football, or fight, and that left hanging around the tennis courts with the girls, listening to them talk about periods and shagging.

Most days he sat quietly between Jess and Lucy, his BFFs, doodling cartoons of them with the bigger boobs they craved, but not today. Nah. Today, he couldn't sit still, and it didn't go unnoticed.

"Bloody hell, Charlie," Jess said as Charlie paced around. "You got ants in your pants, babe?"

Charlie shot her a baleful glare. "Piss off."

"Oooh. Someone's touchy."

"I'm not touchy." But Charlie gave in and drifted back to his usual place all the same. "My parents are taking some new kids. They're coming today."

"Ah. Are you pissed off about it?"

"No, my folks have taken plenty of kids before."

"Then what?"

Charlie shrugged. "Dunno. It's just been a while. Forgotten what it's like to have new people in the house. Mum's been cleaning all week and moving the furniture around. Feels weird."

Jess gave him a cuddle. Across the tennis court, a year-eleven douche shot him the stink eye. Dickhead had been trying to get in Jess's knickers since year nine, and he had it in for Charlie, if the graffiti scrawled on Charlie's locker was anything to go by: *Gaylord Zone*. Ha. If only they knew.

"So," Jess pressed. "How old are these new foster kids? Are they little ones?"

"Not really." Why did people always assume the only kids who needed help were bloody toddlers? "Six and fifteen."

"Boys or girls?"

"One of each. The boy is fifteen."

"Oooh, a boy?"

"Yep." Charlie tried not to notice the flare of curiosity in Jess's gaze. Then he tried to ignore the irritation he felt when he failed. "His name's Leo."

"What does he look like?"

Charlie thought of the photo in his desk drawer and shrugged. "No idea."

"He sounds hot."

"You got that from his name?"

"You can tell a lot about someone by their name."

Charlie snorted. "You've been reading too much *Heat*."

"Better than those crap comics you read."

Charlie grinned. Jess's scowl always made him laugh. Her nose screwed up and made her resemble an angry racoon. And he tried not to think about the odd urge he felt to shield Leo from her attention. Or, as he glanced around the tennis court and took in the gangs of posturing boys and tarted-up girls, anyone else's.

Get a grip, de Sousa. It's not like he'll notice you anyway.

Apart from Charlie's loyal band of girls, and the goons who liked to pull his hair and call him a poof, no one ever did.

Charlie cycled his BMX home at half three. As usual, along the dirt track that cut behind Heyton's town centre, he encountered the gang of year elevens who often heckled as he pedalled past. They didn't let him down today.

"Backs to the wall. Faggy Charlie might jump ya."

Wankers. Though Charlie couldn't deny that they were kind of astute when it came to his sexuality, aside from the jumping, of course. Darren Stroud was the chief idiot, and Charlie wouldn't touch him if he was the last boy on earth.

After running the gauntlet, Charlie usually loitered in the park in a fruitless attempt to convince himself that the whole world didn't think like year eleven's finest, but not today. Today, everyone in the Poulton household had strict instructions to come straight home, except Andy. He was never around on Thursdays, and Kate wanted everything as normal as possible.

But nothing felt normal when Charlie pushed his bike up the garden path and stowed it in the shed. For starters, Fliss was home and downstairs, rather than holed up in her room, living her life on the internet.

Charlie chucked his bag on the kitchen table. "What are you doing here?"

"What do you think?" Fliss opened the fridge and retrieved sausages and a bag of potatoes. "Mum asked me to cook dinner for the new arrivals."

"Only them? Or are you making some for everyone?"

Fliss tossed a glare over her shoulder. "Very funny. Maybe I won't bother with your plate."

It was a hollow threat. Dinnertime was sacred in the

Poulton house, and for all her faults, Fliss was well versed in Kate's compulsion to feed people. "What time are Mum and Dad coming back?"

"Mum called five minutes ago," Fliss said. "They're leaving Swindon now, so a couple of hours. Have you got homework? Mum says you have to do it before dinner."

"What do you care?"

Fliss shot Charlie another sour look. "I don't, but Dad will do his nut if he has to bitch you out in front of the new kids. Just get it done."

A dozen insults crossed Charlie's mind. He uttered none and swiped a Mars bar from the forbidden cupboard, dodging the spoon Fliss chucked his way. On the table, his phone flashed with a new message from Jess.

Are they there yet? Lucy wants a pic!

Charlie rolled his eyes and turned his phone off. "I'm going upstairs."

Fliss grunted, and Charlie left her to it.

Upstairs, he closed his bedroom door and leaned back against it. He had physics homework, but that could wait . . . it could all wait until he'd put the finishing touches to Leo's room. He rummaged under the bed and found the box storing the illustrations he liked enough to keep, but not enough to put on the walls. The Olympic sketches were at the very bottom. He'd drawn them for a school project and never thought of them again until Kate had relayed Fliss's suggestion.

He spread them out on the carpet. Diving, long jump, and boxing: nothing that resembled football in the slightest, save the fact they all featured men in shorts . . . except the diving, of course, which was pretty much—

Stop it.

Charlie caught himself before he got carried away with his pen-and-ink effigy of Tom Daley, and gathered the sports sketches into a pile with a few other random pieces. He considered the small room Kate had kitted out for Leo. There wasn't much to it, but the bed and a tiny chest of drawers. Leo didn't even have a lamp yet. *Fliss has two. I wonder if . . .* Nah. That wouldn't happen. Fliss was toeing the line because Kate and Reg had told her to, but giving away her stuff was never going to happen. Shame, because after Charlie had ventured into the study, clambered on Leo's bed, and tacked the sports posters to the ceiling, Leo's new life still seemed pretty bare.

The rest of the afternoon dragged out in a dull haze of homework. Charlie was falling asleep over the origins of the universe, when Fliss stalked into his room just before six.

"They're nearly here. Remember we're not allowed down till Dad calls us."

"I *know*." Charlie sat up and shoved his homework in his bag. It was standard practice to introduce the family one by one when new kids came, though it had been a while. "I forgot to ask Mum if Lila can speak. Does she?"

"No idea. There's something really bad in their file, though. I caught Mum crying over it last night."

"Crying?"

"Yeah. Not all of us sleep like babies."

That's because some of us get up in the morning. But Charlie kept that to himself. Fliss had a bar job at the pub down the road and seemed to think a few late nights a week gave her license to sleep till noon every day. Not that Charlie cared. Did he want to dodge Fliss in the bathroom every morning? Hell no. "Why was Mum was crying?"

Fliss shrugged. "Dunno. I reckon it's to do with their father, though. I asked Dad where he was. He wouldn't tell me, and I heard him telling Mum he was going to keep his distance from Leo for a while."

"From Leo?" That caught Charlie off guard. Kate and Reg

specialised in caring for girls who'd suffered abuse wherever they'd been before, and he'd half expected Reg to leave Lila mostly to Kate, to start with, at least. But Leo—angry, disillusioned, struggling at school—was the kind of kid that bohemian woodwork teacher Reg lived for. It didn't make any sense. "Why Leo?"

"I don't bloody know. Piss off with the questions, will you? Ask Dad yourself."

Fat chance. Reg had a thing for respecting privacy. If Fliss hadn't been able get it out of him, no one could.

The front door opened. Charlie scrambled from the floor and took a step toward the door before he remembered he had to stay put.

Fliss peered through the window, solving the mystery of why she'd come to Charlie's room in the first place, rather than her converted-attic lair. "Can't see anything. Mum must've brought them in before Dad unloaded the car."

"Let's go down—"

"*No.* Not until they call us. Besides, it doesn't look like there's much stuff in the boot, so it won't be long anyway."

Charlie scowled, and there wasn't much to do but sit on his bed, doodling in his sketchbook and straining his ears, until Reg knocked on the door and summoned Fliss downstairs.

It seemed like a lifetime before he came back for Charlie.

Charlie's frown deepened. "How come Fliss always gets to go first?"

Reg offered a tired smile. "Because that's how we do this, and routine is good for all of us in times of great change."

Charlie grumbled and slid off his bed. "You sound a hundred years old when you talk like that."

"As of today, I have five kids. It's hardly surprising that I sound old. Now, come on. Leo needs rescuing from your mother and Fliss."

Charlie refrained from pointing out that, at twenty-five and nineteen, Andy and Fliss didn't count as kids, and followed Reg downstairs.

Reg stopped at the living room door. "In you go."

"You're not coming?"

"I'm going to finish off dinner," Reg said. "Go on. You can put a film on if you want."

He disappeared into the kitchen. Charlie put his hand on the living room door and felt a strange shot of nerves that quelled the anticipation he'd harboured all day. From his picture, Leo Hendry appeared good-looking and cool, like the hot lads from lower sixth who played football in the park after school, but the longer Charlie had stared at his image, the more something had felt off. Still felt off. The wait to meet his new foster siblings had been unending, but suddenly seemed nowhere near long enough.

The feeling remained as Charlie pushed open the living room door. A stranger by the window turned and met his gaze. *Leo.* Tall and curly-haired, like his picture had promised, he appeared just as Charlie expected, save the bandage that covered his entire left arm, and the emptiest eyes Charlie had ever seen.

<h1 style="text-align:center">THREE</h1>

The new presence in the room irritated Leo. Like it wasn't enough to watch the rest of them pretending that they gave a shit about Lila, now he had to make conversation with some gangly kid—a kid, if he'd understood his new foster-monster correctly, who was going to be his "brother" for the foreseeable future.

Great. Could this day get any worse? Ha. If the last few months had taught Leo anything, it was that things could always get worse.

"Um . . . All right, mate? I'm Charlie."

"I know." Leo flicked his gaze to the arts-and-craft session going on at the far side of the large, open-plan living room—Lila, Kate, and a bird called Fliss, all plaiting stupid pieces of string like it was the best thing in the world—and back to the kid. "Who cares?"

"Fair enough. I'm guessing you're Leo?"

"If you say so." Leo eyed Charlie, who pushed himself off the doorframe and ventured into the room to fiddle with the TV. He was taller than Leo, and lean, like he hadn't quite grown into his legs yet, with olive skin and shiny dark hair. *I wonder what his eyes are like.* For a moment, Leo regretted not bothering to take a proper look, then movement from Lila at the dining table caught his attention.

"*I'm hungry. Dinner soon?*" she signed.

Leo signed back, "*When they tell us where the food is.*"

Lila started to reply, but the foster monster, Kate, rose and waved her hand. She shook her head when she had Lila's attention and signed along with her speech. "We eat together in this house, Leo. Dinner's at seven, but you can have some fruit if you're hungry."

Leo frowned. He was used to sign language being their own secret code. He'd forgotten everyone in this new place probably signed better than he did. "I'm not hungry."

"Okay, sweetie. Let me know if you change your mind."

Kate left the room. She came back with a bowl of grapes for Lila. Leo wanted to cross the room and check they were seedless. Grape seeds irritated the cough Lila had developed since the fire, but something stayed him.

Charlie touched Leo's arm. Leo hadn't noticed him slouching on the arm of the sofa. "Do you want to play Xbox downstairs?"

Leo kept his gaze on Lila, despite a strange urge to acquaint himself with the face attached to the blazing fingertips on his arm. "Downstairs?"

"Yeah, in the cellar with all the games and stuff. Want to see?"

Yes. "No, thanks."

Charlie let his hand drop and glanced over Leo's shoulder. Leo didn't have to turn to know that he'd caught the eye of someone behind them. *Reg, I bet.* The bloke had been lurking like a stalker since he and his wife had turned up at the house of the latest set of foster parents to show Leo the door.

"Um, what about PlayStation?"

"You say 'um' a lot." Leo finally took a proper look at Charlie. Wished he hadn't. Charlie's dark-brown eyes and full lips were a distraction he didn't need. "Have you got a stutter or something?"

"No." Charlie got up and turned away, head down, slender shoulders slumped. Leo almost felt bad, until Charlie stopped, his hand on the door. "I'm going to bring the Wii up. I don't give a shit if you play or not, but anything's got to be better than staring daggers at my mum's back."

Twat.

Charlie left the room. Reg took his place in the doorway. "Charlie's a good kid. With any luck, you'll be going to the same school soon, so it might be good to spend some time together."

"Okay."

Reg raised an eyebrow but said no more. He moved to the table with the others and hovered with his hand on Kate's back. Leo waited for her to jump and move away, but she didn't. In fact, she smiled, which did nothing to calm the burning in Leo's chest. He smelled whiskey and smoke, and the scaly, burned skin began to smoulder as Reg pulled up a chair beside Lila. He reached for the bracelet she was working on, signed something Leo couldn't see.

Then he touched her arm.

Leo jumped up and darted across the room. He wrenched Lila from her chair and tugged her behind him. "Get your hands off her."

Reg pushed his chair back and stood. Leo steeled himself, but instead of advancing on them, Reg retreated to the big bay window and raised his hands. "I wasn't going to hurt her, Leo. No one's going to hurt you here."

The growl in Leo's own throat surprised him. He'd wanted to hit Dennis, but he wanted to hit Reg more. Wanted to wipe that fake, patient stare from his fake, patient face. Wanted to punch him until he punched Leo back and showed his true colours.

He pulled Lila farther behind him and balled his hands into fists. He stepped forward, but Kate blocked his path. She was a petite woman, half the size of his own mother, but her unmoving stance stopped Leo in his tracks.

"Leo, honey. Let Lila go. I'm going to take her upstairs so she can wash her hands for dinner."

She held out her hands. Her smile was kind, but Reg's presence behind her set Leo's teeth on edge. He tightened his grip on Lila. She squirmed and tapped his arm, but he held firm even as a mist descended in his noisy brain. How many times had Dennis torn them apart? Locked Lila in her room so he could punish Leo for putting himself between Dennis and their mother?

"*Leo.*" For the second time that day, Charlie's gentle voice startled him. Charlie put the games console on the arm of the couch and Leo felt his liquid gaze all over him. "Lila's okay. She's safe with Kate."

For a moment, no one moved, or even breathed, but then the fog clouding Leo's vision lifted as abruptly as it had descended.

He let Lila go. Fliss, who'd remained silent until now, left the room. Reg followed, then Kate stepped forward. "I'm going to take Lila upstairs to wash her hands."

Dazed, Leo nodded. He was still getting used to the red haze that misted his vision when his heart beat too fast. "She doesn't like cold water."

"I know, sweetheart. You wrote it in your family journal."

"Why do you have that?"

Kate lifted Lila to her hip as though she weighed nothing at all. "Your caseworker gave it to us. That's why they asked you to keep it, so we could get to know you a little before you got here."

That sounded about right, though Leo had only filled out

the stupid diary so people didn't fuck with Lila's routine while he was at school. "She's allergic to baby wipes too, so don't clean her face with them."

"I know, Leo."

Kate carried Lila out of the room. Leo ran a hand through his hair and tugged hard, using the pain to ground himself. New places always felt weird, but this house was something else. He glanced around at the smiling family photos, bright cushions, and warm wood floors. The big semidetached was the kind of home Leo dreamed of on the rare nights his subconscious took him somewhere pleasant . . . took him to a place where smoke meant campfires and warm beer, not the brutal end of his childhood.

Charlie cleared his throat. Somehow, Leo had missed him setting up the Wii and parking himself on the coffee table. "Wanna play Mario Kart?"

"Hmm?"

"Mario Kart," Charlie said. "Come on. We've got time for a quick game before dinner."

"And dinner's at seven, yeah?"

"Yep." Charlie grinned, and it changed his whole face. His soulful eyes brightened and sucked Leo in, drew him closer until he took a place on the coffee table and found himself falling headfirst into the forgotten world of animated mushrooms and magical gold coins.

The rest of the evening passed in a blur of video games and companionable silence with Charlie, and then dinner at the big round table with everyone else: Kate, Fliss, Charlie . . . Reg. Leo watched Reg like a hawk, but he made no move to touch Lila again.

After dinner, Kate signed to Lila. *"Bath time."*

Leo stood and held out his hand. "I'll do it."

"You don't have to, Leo. It's our job to take care of you and Lila now."

Our job. Leo glanced between Kate and Reg. *No fucking way.* He touched Lila's arm and signed, *"Come."*

No one stopped them. Leo took Lila upstairs to the family bathroom—Reg and Kate had their own—and ran Lila a bath. He tested the water absently while Lila looked on, suspicious of the big, claw-footed tub.

Leo turned the taps off. *"Get in."*

Lila shook her head and bit her bottom lip. *"Don't want to."*

"Why not?"

"Scary."

Leo suppressed a sigh and looked around for a bribe. Lila didn't like change, but pretty things often distracted her. He found a half-empty bottle of bubble bath. *"Bubbles?"*

Lila wrinkled her nose. *"It's too late."*

"So? It smells nice."

"I have a box of old toy ponies under my bed. Do you think she'd like to play with them?"

Leo glanced over his shoulder. Fliss, the oldest foster kid, stood in the doorway. "Why do you have toys under your bed?"

"Why not?"

Leo didn't have an answer to that. He turned his back on Fliss and shrugged. "Lila likes horses."

"I'll get them, then."

He heard her go, and it seemed like no time at all had passed before she was back with a pink plastic box.

Fliss stopped in the doorway again and held them out. "They're a bit manky now, but they used to be my favourite bath toys. Dad still teases me for lining them up in size order."

Leo took the box and signed to Lila, *"You can play with them in the bath."*

Then he looked back at Fliss. "Who's your dad?"

Lila fumbled with the box lid. Fliss moved to help before Leo thought to stop her. "Reg is my dad, at least the only one I've ever known. He and Kate took me in when I was two."

If Leo remembered right, Fliss was twenty now. Eighteen years. Fuck. "Why do you live here and not by yourself?"

"Because this is my home, and the real world sucks arse."

A grin escaped Leo before he could stop it. He watched Lila dig the best ponies out of the box and place them carefully in the water, then he considered his new foster sister. With her blonde hair and pale skin, she didn't resemble Charlie, though she was equally gorgeous.

Leo frowned. When had he decided Charlie was gorgeous? Not that it mattered, because Charlie *was* gorgeous and—

"Leo?" Fliss held out her hands to help Lila into the bath. "Is this okay?"

Leo shrugged, but Lila hesitated, her eyes on Leo. "*Go on,*" he signed. "*Get in.*"

"You're really good with her," Fliss remarked when Lila was settled. "Have you always looked after her like this?"

Leo knelt at the side of the bath. "No. I didn't need to before."

Fliss nodded like she knew. Perhaps she did. Leo had seen the ever-growing files that followed him and Lila wherever they went. Maybe Fliss had too. Or perhaps she had her own file of darkness and death.

Lila splashed Leo's arm. "*Play with me.*"

Leo picked up a pony, a pink one with glittery hair. "*Name?*"

Lila shrugged and pointed at Fliss. "*Ask her.*"

"*You ask.*"

"*Sparkles,*" Fliss signed. She picked up another pony and carefully finger-spelled the name.

Leo snorted, though he was glad that Fliss had tackled that sign for him. "Captain America?"

"Hey, don't blame me." Fliss rolled her eyes. "This one's Charlie's. He used to love that Marvel crap. He's into some weird Japanese rubbish these days."

Leo didn't know why he cared, but he filed the Charlie-themed snippet away for future reference. "Thanks for lending us the ponies."

"No worries." Fliss stood and dried her hands. "Don't tell Mum I said this, but I quite like it when they take little ones like Lila. Gives me an excuse to get all the pink shit out. Oh, and Leo?"

"Yeah?"

"Don't give Reg a hard time. He's a good man—the best—and if I see you squaring up to him again, I'll deck you myself."

It was late by the time Leo left Lila for the night. Her new bedroom had unsettled her, and she'd only fallen asleep when Leo had crawled under her duvet.

He'd crept away to find Kate watching from the top of the stairs.

"Well done, Leo. It's not easy getting a young one to sleep when they're in a new place."

"We're used to it." Leo stepped around Kate. "She'll be okay in a few days."

Kate didn't call him out on the fib, though she must've known about Lila's night wanderings. "What about you, honey? Do you want a hot drink before you go to bed?"

"No, thanks." Leo looked around the landing for a place to sit and listen for Lila.

Like she'd read his mind, Kate touched his good arm, though

her hand didn't linger. "Our bedroom is right there. Reg will hear Lila if she wakes up."

"Yeah, and then what will he do?"

"He'll wake me," Kate said. "Leo, I know you're nervous, but you have nothing to fear from anyone here. We're going to take care of you, for as long as you need us."

"We don't need you."

Leo made his escape to the door at the end of the landing. For a moment, he thought Kate might follow, but she didn't. Instead, he heard her pull Lila's door ajar and go into the bathroom.

He stepped into his own room, shut the door, and sagged against it, more relieved than he cared to admit. He'd had enough playing nice, and it was only the first day.

Exhausted, he made his way to the bed he'd dumped his bag on earlier that day. His hands were shaking, like they had done since he'd spotted Reg's car pulling onto the driveway of the old foster place. *Damn it.* He shoved them in his pockets. That home had been a crock of shit. Behaviour charts, cleaning rotas, and endless lists of rules . . .

Speaking of which . . .

Leo eyed the closed bedroom door and wondered how long it would be before Kate or Reg came in and turned the lights off. How long he'd last before he told them to stick it too. In his pockets, he clenched his fists so tight his nails bit into his palms. Three years left until he could take Lila and get a flat of their own. A safe place where *he* made the rules, and they could keep the lights on all night if they wanted to.

Yeah, 'cause it's Lila who's afraid of the dark.

The door opened. Leo steeled himself for Kate or Reg, but it was Charlie.

"All right?"

Leo nodded and went back to staring at the ceiling.

Charlie hovered in the doorway. "Do you need to put any of your stuff in my wardrobe?"

"What?"

"Your stuff," Charlie repeated. "You don't have much storage in here."

Leo had forgotten that, even though Kate had blathered on about it most of the way home. And now he surveyed the tiny, sparse room, he decided that it suited him. He shook his head without glancing Charlie's way. "I'm fine, thanks."

"Suit yourself."

Charlie left—irritatingly leaving the door open—though it didn't sound like he'd gone far. Leo listened to him move around for a while, before his gaze drifted from the ceiling to the window. The glass reflected across the hallway, picking up Charlie's lean form as he moved around his own room, half-undressed in what, in soft focus, looked like pyjama bottoms.

Damn. Leo's chest warmed as he took in Charlie's sinewy, tanned back and lanky arms. His shower-damp hair and prominent hip bones.

Yep.

Definitely gorgeous.

He searched the room for something—anything—to distract him. The walls were mostly bare, except for a few strange cartoons that were randomly dotted on the ceiling, some cut from magazines and others hand drawn. His gaze fell on a drawing at the foot of the bed, a felt-tip pen sketch of a red-haired woman with huge eyes and a pointy chin. Despite her exaggerated features, Leo could tell the woman was supposed to be Kate. Before he knew what he was doing, He sat up and pried it gently from the wall, then took it to Charlie's open door. "Is this the Japanese stuff that Fliss was talking about?"

"'Stuff'?" Charlie glanced over his shoulder. "Don't be polite on her behalf."

Leo said nothing. He'd liked Fliss's blunt way of speaking, even when she'd threatened to kick his head in. It was a threat he'd heard a thousand times over, but coming from Fliss with her pretty eyes and box of ponies, it'd been oddly reassuring. A flash of normality in a strange new world.

"It's manga," Charlie said when Leo let the silence fill the room like a dense black fog. "I draw them with my mate Jess. She writes the storyboards."

"Then what do you do with them?"

Charlie shrugged. "Stick 'em on our bedroom walls, mainly. I'm saving some for my uni applications, though. I want to go to UAL."

Uni. So Charlie was one of those kids with plans . . . prospects, a future. Leo wanted to hate him. Couldn't. "Is manga like that anime stuff?"

"God, no." Charlie moved so fast he blurred across the room. He crouched down by his bed and rummaged underneath. "Anime is totally different. Look."

Leo blinked, taken aback by Charlie's sudden animation and the stacks of weird comic books he produced from under the bed. He stepped forward, curious, despite the heavy haze of apathy clouding his mind. "Which is which?"

"This one is manga . . . this one anime screenshot." Charlie pointed between two images that appeared pretty similar to Leo. "See the difference in the detail? Anime uses loads of effects and music. Manga is all about the illustrations."

Leo studied the drawings. He didn't know jack about art, but the fiery gleam in Charlie's dark eyes made him feel a little dizzy. "So manga is comics and anime is . . . like, um, animated stuff?"

"Something like that." Charlie huffed out an irritated puff of air and shoved his boxes back under the bed. "I'm knackered. All right if I turn the light off?"

Leo swallowed. He'd noticed the single lamp by Charlie's bed and fought the urge to swipe it. "Whatever. Are we allowed to use the shower at night?"

"Course we are." Charlie shot Leo a strange look, turned off the light, and crawled into his bed. "But don't leave wet towels on the floor. Mum goes mental when we do that."

"She's not my mum." Leo backed away. In the murky dark of the room, he could just about see Charlie's face, see him watching Leo like he was a stray dog, likely to turn at any moment. "Where are the towels?"

"In the airing cupboard, mate."

Mate, sweetheart, darling, honey. Over the course of the evening, Leo had heard them all. "Don't call me that."

"Call you what?"

"*Mate*. It's not my name."

"Oh." Charlie's voice was hollow. "Sorry. It's a habit. You want me to just call you Leo?"

"I *am* Leo. Why would you call me anything else?"

"Fair enough."

Leo almost felt bad again, but it passed. The fire had taken everything—home, things, Wendy's still-warm body. In this strange house, surrounded by strangers, Leo's name was all he and Lila had left.

He retreated from Charlie's dark room and went to the bathroom, peeking into Lila's bedroom on his way. She was sound asleep, and didn't stir as he rescued the hand she'd wedged between the wall and the bed, and tucked her favourite bear in beside her.

In the bathroom, he took a shower, slathered ointment on his scarred skin, and redressed his arm with the fresh bandages someone had left out. He didn't look at the mangled flesh—never did, unless he felt like making himself retch—and then, despite an urge to leave a mess just for the hell of it, he dumped his wet towel in the washing basket.

Back on the landing, he noted that the house had stilled while he'd been in the shower, and the only sign of life now was the sliver of light filtering through Kate and Reg's open bedroom door. He checked Lila one last time, then slunk back to his own room where the dark enveloped him. The silence was heavy—choking—and he wondered if Charlie was asleep.

Charlie.

A shiver passed through Leo. Charlie was as annoying as the rest of the world, but Leo felt somehow colder without his warm, earnest gaze following him, and disquiet gnawed in the pit of his stomach. His pulse quickened and his breath caught, like he'd played ninety minutes on a football pitch without moving a muscle. Sweat prickled his shower-damp skin. He bit down hard on his bottom lip and rummaged in his bag. Nights were often like this—a long, anxious wait for Lila to wake up, and then an even longer wait for morning to come, rocking her in his arms while she slept, hopefully comforted, for a while, from the bad dreams that plagued them both.

Only one thing ever calmed his own wayward nerves, and he found it hidden in a sock at the bottom of the bag that held his worldly possessions. He retrieved the small bag of weed and crawled out of his bedroom window and onto the porch roof.

He rolled a joint and lit up, blowing clouds of fragrant smoke to the sky, and letting the earthy scent seep into his bones, calming him from the inside out. He closed his eyes and thought of Wendy. Sometimes he imagined that he saw her behind the moon, giving him the look that made him squirm and do anything but meet her gaze. The frown that let him know he was in deep trouble. He'd hated that look before it had been gone forever.

Now he'd do anything to see it again.

FOUR

It was still dark when Charlie woke the next day. Winter was like that: gloomy and misty, the fog swirling around the streetlight by the window. An orange glow filtered through the half-shut curtains. His eyes tracked the light down to the open door and found a bright-green gaze staring right back at him.

Charlie sat up. He'd forgotten about his new housemates, but it wasn't Leo who waved at him, it was little Lila.

Startled, Charlie waved too and signed, "*Morning.*"

"*Hello,*" Lila signed back. "*I'm hungry.*"

"*Oh.*" The rest of the house, including Leo, seemed to be fast asleep. Charlie considered his options, and signed, "*Breakfast?*"

Lila nodded and disappeared onto the landing, coughing. Charlie hurriedly got up and followed her, poking his head into Leo's room. Lila's soft toys littered the bed all around his sleeping form, like she'd spent all night there—perhaps she had, and Charlie wondered how often Leo shared his bed with Lila. And how Lila had snuck down the hallway without Reg hearing.

Charlie darted back into his room, snagged a hoodie, and

then followed Lila downstairs, ready to grab her if she stumbled. He thought about taking her hand, but a flashback to Leo's fury at Reg the previous evening stopped him.

He doesn't like people touching Lila.

Charlie considered why, but killed the thought before it could take hold. He'd seen enough in the Poulton house to know that there were many stories that he didn't need to hear.

In the kitchen, they found Reg already seated at the kitchen table. Charlie frowned. It was 6 a.m., and no one in the family was an early riser. "What are you doing up?"

Reg stood and put the kettle on to boil. "Leo was creeping around until all hours, then I heard Lila get up. I didn't want to disturb them once they finally settled, so I came down and scrabbled through some of the work I missed yesterday."

Charlie eyed the tools spread on the table. Reg taught woodwork at Heyton College when he wasn't collecting stray children from social services. "Are you working today?"

"Not today. Your mother and I are taking Leo and Lila to the doctor."

"Why?"

Reg smiled tiredly. "To register them and have them checked over."

And the rest. But Charlie didn't say it. Instead, he opened the cereal cupboard and beckoned Lila, who'd been hovering behind him since they'd entered the kitchen, over to choose her breakfast. "*Which one?*"

Lila studied the cupboard that Kate had stocked with more choices than usual and pointed at the Coco Pops.

Charlie retrieved the box, but Lila continued to stare into the cupboard. A tiny frown creased her forehead. Charlie glanced at Reg, who was watching them intently, studying . . . analysing, like he always did new kids. He nodded, so Charlie crouched at Lila's side and signed, "*Do you want something else?*"

Lila coughed again and pointed at an unopened box of Shreddies. "*I don't like those.*"

"*Okay. You don't have to eat them.*"

Lila shook her head. "*I don't like them.*"

Something in her posture seemed to make Reg move. He appeared behind Charlie and stepped carefully around him, a move Charlie didn't understand until he realised Reg had avoided approaching Lila directly.

Reg pulled the offending cereal from the cupboard and signed, "*Throw them away?*"

"*In the bin?*" Lila didn't seem convinced, but she didn't seem afraid of Reg. Or hostile, like Leo.

"*Yes,*" Reg signed. "*The big bin outside, if you like?*"

Lila nodded. Reg opened the backdoor and instructed Lila to find her shoes. She ghosted into the hallway as Charlie shot Reg a quizzical frown. "What was all that about?"

Reg shrugged. "We can't fix much in this life, son, but we can chuck out the bloody Shreddies."

Lila came back before Charlie could answer. Reg pointed her in the direction of the nearby wheelie bin and talked her through disposing of the cereal. The whole scene took less than two minutes to play out, but Charlie felt like he'd been dropped into another world.

He poured Lila a bowl of Coco Pops while Reg made tea. Lila ate with her head down, and didn't look up until her bowl was empty.

Charlie picked at his toast and watched her glance around the cosy kitchen. Kate had decorated the whole house in comforting shades, and the AGA kept the kitchen warm in the winter. *I wonder what their old home was like.*

Reg tapped the table to get Lila's attention. "*Drawing?*"

Lila's solemn gaze brightened. "*Can I?*"

"*Of course,*" Reg signed. "Charlie, do you think Lila could use of your special pens? She's a little beyond the crayons we got for her."

No one was allowed to touch Charlie's precious wooden manga pens. He'd saved his paper-round money for six months to buy them. He opened his mouth to protest that there were plenty of art supplies stashed in the study upstairs, but hurried footsteps on the stairs distracted him.

Leo burst into the kitchen. He was beside Lila in an instant, shielding her from Reg's view. "What are you doing?"

"Having breakfast," Reg said mildly. "Lila's had some Coco Pops, now she's going to borrow Charlie's pens to draw more of the daisies she drew so beautifully yesterday. Do you want a cuppa?"

Reg retreated to the kettle without waiting for Leo's response. He didn't even look back, like he couldn't feel Leo's sharp, defensive glare boring into him. Charlie shivered. Something in Leo changed when Reg was around. It was frightening . . . disturbing, and Lila obviously felt it too.

She touched Leo's hand. Charlie couldn't see what she signed, but Leo's expression softened.

"*Yes,*" he signed. "*Use the pens.*"

Charlie took his cue and fetched the pens from his school bag. When he returned, no one had moved. Reg still had his back to Leo, and Leo was still watching him like a sniper. Charlie dropped the case of pens on the table and grabbed scrap paper from the arts-and-crafts box on the dresser. "I want to draw too. What shall we draw?"

Leo cut his gaze at Charlie. "Lila can't hear what you're saying."

"I'm talking to you." Charlie reclaimed his seat at the table and signed, "*No fun on your own.*"

Lila smiled and pulled a sheet of paper toward her. Charlie emptied the pens onto the table. "Dad? Do you want to draw too?"

Reg finally turned around. "Not now, Charlie. I'm going to jump in the shower before Fliss hogs all the hot water. How about the three of you do something nice for the fridge door? We haven't had anything new for ages."

He left the room. Charlie heard his soft tread on the stairs and turned his attention to Leo. "You can sit down now. He's gone."

Leo scowled so hard he looked as though his head might explode. "He doesn't scare me."

"I know," Charlie said. "Why would he? It's his job to take care of you."

"Why do you talk like him?"

"Talk like Reg?"

"Who else?" Leo took a small swig from Lila's juice cup. "You sound just like him when you spout stupid crap like that."

Someone else would perhaps have been offended, or at the least affronted, but Charlie was used to Fliss's sharp tongue. "It's not crap. It's the truth. Reg is the coolest dad around. He'll let you do anything you want if you stick to the house rules."

Leo snorted. "Fuck the rules."

Charlie suppressed a sigh. Late last night, Leo had been given his own copy of the printed list stuck to every bedroom door, and Charlie had seen it shredded in the bathroom bin when he'd brushed his teeth. "Suit yourself. You're going to be pretty bloody bored cooped up here when you break them all."

Leo didn't answer, and Charlie's patience wore thin. He blocked Leo out and returned his focus to Lila, who had sketched a formation of flowers. Charlie studied them, impressed. Neat and intricate, they were better than half the crap his classmates produced at school.

Charlie found some bright colours and pushed them Lila's way. *"Colour them."*

Lila got stuck in. She was halfway through her second flower when Leo pulled out a chair and sat down. Charlie eyed him. For all his belligerence, Leo appeared lost. And tired too, like he hadn't slept in days. Reg had looked much the same, but the strain of fatigue hadn't seemed out of place on his already lined face. On Leo, it didn't feel right at all.

"Do you want any breakfast?"

"Hmm?" Leo glanced up from Lila's work.

"Breakfast," Charlie repeated. "Mum will probably cook for you, as it's your first morning, but I can make you some toast now?"

Leo blinked and rubbed his arm, the arm covered by a thick bandage. "I don't want her to cook for me."

"Have some toast, then. Marmite or jam?"

Leo frowned. Charlie got up anyway and stuck two slices of bread in the toaster. When they were done, he buttered them and left them plain. Leo didn't seem to notice.

"Eat," Charlie said. "If nothing else, it'll keep Mum off your back till lunchtime."

Leo ate slowly, like he wasn't sure of his actions, or if his limbs belonged to him. He seemed surprised when his plate was empty, and Charlie tried not to stare. Eyes half closed, hair tousled from sleep, Leo was beautiful, but that wasn't what was keeping Charlie's attention. No. It was the darkness in that hooded gaze and the weary slump in his posture. It was *wrong*, and Charlie couldn't let it go. "Are you okay?"

Leo cast a dull glance in Charlie's direction. "What?"

"You don't look very well," Charlie said. "Mum's taking you to the doctor today. You should tell her if you feel sick."

"I don't feel sick."

"Yeah? What's up, then? It's not that bad here, honest. Even Fliss likes it."

Leo started to smile, Charlie was almost sure of it, then Kate bustled into the kitchen, and the moment passed.

"Good morning, boys." Kate stopped in front of Lila and signed, "*Good morning. Did you sleep well?*"

Lila started to answer, but Leo pushed his chair back, wooden legs scraping the tiled floor with a flat shriek. "She slept fine."

He pulled Lila from her seat and towed her from the room, leaving her daises abandoned on the kitchen table. Charlie watched them go and tried to figure out what was worse—the disappointment in Kate's gaze, the confusion in Lila's, or the black emptiness in Leo's.

Or the sight of his favourite purple pen disappearing up the stairs.

Leo watched Charlie pedal his bike down the street. Charlie's BMX was blue, like one Leo had once had, but he'd decorated it with weird Japanese stickers and symbols. Combined with his skinny jeans, emo hoodie, and crazy dark hair, he looked a little strange. Not a bad strange, though. Where Leo came from, all the boys were the same: baggy jeans, football, and hair gel. Rinse and repeat.

Leo thought of his old friends. *Do they ever think about me?*

"Leo?" Kate knocked on Leo's bedroom door. "Are you ready, honey? It's time to go."

Leo suppressed a sigh and tore his gaze from the window. Charlie was long gone anyway. "What kind of doctor are you taking us to?"

"Just our GP this morning, but you have an appointment at

the hospital with the burn specialist this afternoon. Reg is going to take you to that one."

"Reg?"

"Yes. I'll be taking care of Lila."

Leo swallowed. He didn't know which was worse: having a hard-faced doctor prod at his ruined skin, or spending the afternoon with creepy Reg.

He followed Kate downstairs. Reg was already in the car, but Lila was waiting by the door.

"*Hurry up,*" she signed. "*Baking cakes when we get back.*"

Leo found a smile from the pit of his stomach and plastered it on his face. "*Not me. I have to see another doctor.*"

He took Lila's hand and led her to Reg's car. She poked him. "*Why? Your poorly arm?*

Leo nodded. Lila had never seen the mangled flesh on his arm, but she knew it was there. A few days after the fire, she'd told him she could still smell it burning. Leo strapped her into the car. He felt sick and dizzy, like he didn't know which way was up, and most days, he smelt it too, awake, asleep . . . always.

The doctor's surgery was a twenty-minute drive away. The doctor was a young Asian woman who listened to Lila's chest and gave her a sticker. Lila smiled like she hadn't smiled in months, and skipped back to Kate, who took her outside and left Leo alone with the doctor.

The doctor ran through the checks Leo had come to expect. Until the fire, he hadn't seen a doctor in years. Recently it seemed like he saw one every bloody day.

"So, Leo. How are you settling into your new foster home?"

Leo forced himself to meet the doctor's gaze. "We only got here yesterday."

"And you were in Swindon before?"

"Yeah."

The doctor made a note, though Leo couldn't see why it

mattered. "I read in your file that you've had trouble sleeping since the accident."

"It wasn't an accident." Leo's temper flared. Why couldn't people call it what it was? "My dad killed my mum."

The doctor didn't blink. "I can give you a mild sedative to help you sleep. A short-term measure until we can arrange proper counselling. I've referred you to a specialist at St. David's."

"St. David's?"

"It's a mental health unit at the hospital, for children and young adults. You've been through a lot, Leo. There's quite a waiting list, but they can help you."

They can help you. Apathy washed over Leo. How many times had he heard those words before any of this shit had happened? Teachers. Police. Social workers. Help . . . yeah right. Too little too late.

Leo stood and shrugged into his coat. "I'm fine, thanks. I don't need any help."

He claimed the prescription slip the doctor held out, though, and escaped to the waiting room.

Reg took the slip from him and scanned the information. He frowned. "Did you ask for these?"

Leo thought about saying he had, just to see that frown deepen, but he couldn't be bothered. "No. She said since I have trouble sleeping, I should take them."

"Do you think you need them?"

"I don't care." Leo took Lila's hand and walked out of the surgery.

A few hours later found Leo trapped in a tiny room with yet

another doctor—a man this time, a white one, with cold hands and bad breath.

The doctor unwound Leo's dressing twisted the arm this way and that. "This is healing nicely," he said. "I'm still concerned about this graft, though. Do you see where it's raised here?"

Leo glanced at the bumpy flesh where the inside of his bicep had been grafted to the outside. Regretted it. The skin felt numb now, like it had ever since the surgery to close the burned hole in his arm, but he hated looking at it. "Do you have to do it again?"

"Perhaps. I think the graft has slipped slightly, but the overall healing is good. I'm reluctant to mess around with it at this stage, but we'll keep an eye on it. Are you all right? You're a little pale."

Leo swallowed the bile in his mouth. "I'm fine."

The doctor said something. Leo didn't quite hear him. Then someone put a hand on his shoulder. It took him a while to realise it was Reg.

"Ah, there you are," he said. "You had a wobble on us, lad."

My name's Leo.

"What's that?" Reg said.

Leo blinked rapidly. Had he said that out loud? He straightened up from where he appeared to have slumped in his chair. "What happened?"

"You fainted. Did you eat breakfast this morning?"

Leo thought back to the toast Charlie had dumped in front of him. "Yeah. Charlie made me toast."

Reg smiled. "Sounds like Charlie. Hmm, perhaps you're dehydrated, then. Have some water."

He held a plastic cup of water to Leo's lips. Leo took a tentative sip and noted they were alone in the doctor's room. He shrugged away from Reg's hands. *Get the fuck off me.* "Where's Dr. Frankenstein?"

"Discussing your case with another doctor. He doesn't want to operate again, so he's hoping the graft will right itself."

"He told you that?"

"Yes, Leo. We're your guardians, for the time being, at least. We want to let you make your own decisions as much as we can, but we can only do that if we know what's going on. You understand that, don't you?"

Leo opened his mouth. Shut it. He understood the words, and even the sentiment, but the power of speech was beyond him. He was going to be sick.

———

Charlie hovered in Leo's doorway, transfixed by the humped shape in the bed. *Still?* Leo had been asleep when Charlie came home from school. He'd missed dinner, and Lila's bath time, and now it was ten o'clock and he'd yet to stir.

No one had mentioned his absence downstairs. Kate had kept Lila close all evening until her bedtime, and it was only then that she'd asked for Leo. Charlie hadn't seen what Kate signed, and something had stopped him from asking her to repeat it. Fliss had taken Lila to bed, and after a restless evening, the entire household had called it an early night.

Charlie leaned on the doorframe, taking comfort in the cool, peeling paint against his cheek. Leo and Lila had been with them for less than forty-eight hours, but everything already felt different. Kate and Reg. The house. Even Fliss. The world had shifted, but Charlie couldn't figure out why. He took a shaky breath and stared at Leo, like he could see through his skin and decipher the boy behind the sullen glares, occasional smirks, and the sad smiles he saved for Lila.

What happened to you?

The unspoken question went unanswered. Leo was curled on his side, his bandaged arm cradled close to his body, like it had been since Charlie had first peeked in on him after school. Charlie gazed a moment longer, before he admitted defeat and returned to his own room, seeking solace in the dark.

A strange noise woke him sometime later. He sat up on his elbows and blinked away sleep. Then he waited, unsure of what had woken him, but silence reigned. There was nothing to be heard save the arthritic creak of the central heating pipes.

Charlie lay back down, unnerved. He usually slept like the dead, convinced he'd blinked and the night had melted into a new day. He closed his eyes. Lethargy washed over him. He was halfway to sleep when he heard it again . . . a soft moan that cut through the stillness of the house and gave him goose bumps.

Alarmed, he scrambled out of bed and across the landing. In the murky darkness he could hardly make Leo out, but the moan had come from him, Charlie felt it in his bones, and when Leo cried out again, he was across the room before he knew he'd moved.

But he faltered at Leo's bedside. Even in sleep, Leo's demeanour told the world he didn't want to be touched. Charlie crouched down and absorbed the tremble beneath Leo's skin, and it shuddered through him.

Why am I shaking with him?

Charlie had no answer to that. Maybe he should say something, but what? Leo didn't seem the type to be easily comforted, and Charlie didn't know how anyway. Instead he sat on the floor and leaned back on Leo's bed. It was a while before he realised Leo was staring right at him.

FIVE

"Splash me a fag, mate?"

The boy in the bomber jacket eyed Leo suspiciously, like every other person at Heyton High had since he'd walked through the gates that morning. A new kid on the block was apparently big news, but Leo didn't much care. Bollocks to them. All of them. He was only here 'cause he couldn't stand another day stuck at home dodging Kate's smothering affection.

And you want to be where Charlie is . . .

Wherever that was. Leo hadn't seen Charlie since they'd parted ways at the school's reception that morning, Charlie to his tutor group, and Leo to a meeting with the head of year ten.

Charlie, Charlie, Charlie.

Get a grip. Leo tried to tune out the devil on his shoulder. Focussed on the kid who was buckling under the weight of Leo's patented blank stare and reaching for his battered packet of Mayfair.

Charlie, Charlie, Charlie.

His deep brown eyes.

His endless long limbs.

His gentle, probing gaze when Leo had woken a few nights ago from the worst nightmare he'd had in months.

In the darkness, Charlie had scrambled back to the doorway the moment he'd realised Leo was awake, and they'd hardly spoken since—at least, Leo hadn't—but Leo hadn't forgotten it. Hadn't forgotten lying awake for hours after, and feeling the roiling turmoil in his belly calm with every slow whisper of Charlie's breath.

"Do you want a fag or not?"

Leo cut his gaze to the kid proffering his open pack of smokes. The cigarette in the back row was turned upside down for luck. Wendy had always done that, saved it till the end, promising it would be the last one before she gave up for good. No one had ever believed her. Leo claimed the smoke next to it, took a lighter from his new friend, and lit up. He glanced around as he blew smoke into the grey sky. The tennis courts at Heyton High were teeming with teenagers, the boys playing football, fighting, or smoking. The girls standing around in groups, watching . . . seeing everything, like girls always did.

"So who the fuck are you, anyway?"

Leo cast a bored glance to his left. "Leo. Who are you?"

"Wayne, innit. Think I saw you in physics this morning. I'm gonna jump the fence and get some chips. Wanna come?"

Not particularly. Leo hadn't been hungry since he'd started taking the pills the GP had given him. They hadn't done much to help him sleep, but late at night while he waited for Lila to join him, he found himself enjoying the scratchy, numbing buzz that tickled his brain.

Still, with forty-five minutes left of lunchtime, he had nothing better to do, so he followed Wayne across the tennis courts to the school boundary and considered the fence. It was seven foot high with plenty of handholds to aid a quick scramble over the top. An easy feat six months ago, but now? Leo flexed his damaged arm. He hadn't tested his weakened muscles since the fire, hadn't cared enough to bother, but suddenly, with the fence right in front of him, he couldn't wait a moment longer.

Hungry or not, he *had* to get to the other side.

Mindful of Wayne watching, he stuck his smoke in his mouth and launched the messenger bag Kate had bought him over the fence. It landed in a bush, upside down, zips swinging in the wind. *That could be you in a minute.* Leo pictured himself careening through the air and landing smack on the concrete below. He imagined the impact. Felt it spread through him, cracking his bones—

"Are you coming or what?"

Leo blinked. Lost in his morbid imagination, he'd missed Wayne clearing the fence.

Get on with it, dickhead.

He took a few steps back and braced himself for the run up. His footsteps pounded the tarmac, the metal links of the fence bit into his hands, and then he was flying over the top, the wind in his ears, and he hardly felt the tearing burn in his left arm.

He hit the ground. Shockwaves travelled up his legs from the balls of his feet, but he remained upright. Breathless, but upright. For a moment he wanted to cry, mourning the loss of his imagined fall, then exhilaration hit him and he wanted to jump all over again.

Then he met Wayne's bored gaze and reality seeped into him. *Chips, remember?*

Leo sloped to the bush and retrieved his bag. Wayne offered him another smoke. He took it and followed Wayne to the local chippie, a place that looked and smelled like arse.

No, thanks. Leo waited outside and took in Heyton's high street. Manky chip shop aside, the town was far more glamorous than the grey streets of Swindon—posher people, flashier cars. He watched the world go by and pretended he was waiting for

Wendy to emerge from one of the poncy coffee shops across the road, the one with the vintage cake stands, and the grand piano in the window. Then his fantasy faltered. Eyes closed to the world, he could picture Kate in a place like that, with her flowing skirts and dangly earrings, but not Wendy. Life with Dennis had hardened her, and pretty things had often passed her by.

Wayne emerged from the chip shop with a grunt. He offered Leo his soggy bag of chips, but Leo looked away. "Nah, mate. You have 'em."

"Suit yourself." Wayne turned back the way they'd come. "So where are you from, anyway? You sound Irish or some shit."

"Irish? Piss off. I'm from Swindon."

Wayne was apparently mystified, like he'd never ventured beyond his own back garden. Perhaps he hadn't. "What did you come here for? Did you move house?"

"Something like that."

Wayne let it go, apparently not one for small talk, which suited Leo. He'd argued his case to come to school in order to escape the searching conversations every fucker at home seemed to want.

They drifted the rest of the way back in silence. Leo relieved Wayne of a few more fags, but the jaunt remained unremarkable, save the vexed teacher waiting for them at the gate.

The teacher let them in, and then fixed Wayne with a frown Leo had seen from just about every teacher he'd ever known. "Been somewhere nice, Mr. Murphy?"

Wayne shrugged and tossed his chip paper into a nearby bin. "Showing the new kid where the good grub was, weren't I?"

"Very funny. You know you're not allowed off school property at lunchtime anymore. We stopped that last term."

"Did you? Sorry, miss. I forgot."

For a moment, Leo thought the teacher would let them go, but then her gaze flickered briefly to Leo and something clicked in her expression. "Leaving school property without permission counts as truanting. Go and wait for me in my office. I'm sure your mother will be over the moon to have you suspended again."

Wayne shuffled off with an insolent roll of his eyes, and Leo wondered if Wayne's record was as blighted as his own.

"I've never seen you before. You must be new," the teacher said. "First day?"

Leo shrugged. Stuff talking to teachers. Nosy bastards, all of them.

"Well, even so, young man, I know you were told this morning that students aren't allowed off-site. What do you have to say for yourself?"

Nothing that wouldn't get him in more trouble, and it turned out not to matter.

"Um, Mrs. Parkin? This is Leo, my new foster brother."

The teacher—Mrs. Parkin, apparently—and Leo both looked around to find Charlie behind him, hair a mess, and a dark-blue hoodie over his school-issue blazer. Charlie met Leo's gaze briefly, then focussed on the teacher again.

"Leo came in with me this morning. He didn't have an induction."

That wasn't strictly true. Leo had been spared the student-led orientation Charlie had warned him about on the way to school, but he'd still endured an hour-long lecture from Mr. Donnelly, head of year ten. Did Charlie know, or care, that he'd known perfectly well that leaving school at lunchtime was against the rules?

Mrs. Parkin eyed Charlie. Her expression softened, like she was fond of him, and then it changed, like she'd remembered something long forgotten.

She knows.

Fuck.

She knows.

It always happened like this. Teachers, doctors, social workers—Leo could always tell when they knew. They looked at him differently, like Wendy had looked at the dead cat he'd found by the river. Mrs. Parkin touched his arm, and he jumped back like he'd been burned all over again, stumbled, and cold sweat beaded his back. "Don't touch me."

Mrs. Parkin raised her hands. "All right. I was just saying you're free to go. Charlie says you have art together next lesson. I suggest you make your way there and keep your nose clean from now on."

Leo blinked. *"Charlie says you have art together."* When had he said that?

"And take that sweatshirt off, Mr. de Sousa."

"Yes, miss." Charlie tugged Leo's good arm, like he knew the other was throbbing, burning . . . smouldering. "Come on, Leo. Let's go."

Leo let Charlie tow him away from the searching gaze of Mrs. Parkin. His heart slowed with every step and embarrassment replaced the heady rush of fear. "You know we're not really brothers, don't you?"

Charlie rolled his eyes. "Don't worry. I'm not going to tell anyone."

"Tell anyone what?"

"That we know each other."

Charlie turned away before Leo could answer, and disappeared into a nearby art room. Lacking any better ideas, Leo followed him and found the lesson had already started.

The teacher met him at the door. "You must be Leo. Take a seat next to Charlie. I'll get you a book and some pencils."

Leo followed the teacher's gaze to where Charlie was sitting at the back of the classroom, head down, already engrossed in whatever he was working on. There was an empty stool beside him. Deliberate? Stuff it. After a day of being stuck beside a bunch of numpties, Leo didn't much care.

He made his way across the classroom and dropped onto the stool. The teacher placed a sketchbook and a few pencils on the bench. "Charlie can fill you in on what we're doing."

The teacher walked away without another word. Leo watched him go. That was a new one. Most teachers had bent his ear for twenty minutes before they'd let him sit down.

"We're sketching the view through the window," Charlie said. "You can draw the science block to the left, or the memorial garden to the right."

Leo peered at Charlie's sketchbook. "What are you drawing?"

"The duck in the pond."

"Where's the pond?"

Charlie shrugged. "Who cares?"

Leo grinned. Finally. A sentiment he could relate to. "How come your name is de Sousa? Thought you'd have taken Reg's name by now."

"Why would you think that?" Charlie kept his gaze on his work. "You hate Reg, remember?"

"Says who?"

"Says you. Yesterday."

"Didn't."

"Yes, you did. After he gave you your school blazer. You called him a prick and told him you hated him."

Oops. Leo had muttered the words under his breath when he'd been halfway upstairs. He'd forgotten Charlie had been behind him. "So? Doesn't mean you hate him too. Call him 'Daddy' don't you?"

"Not always. Sometimes I call him Reg, and he doesn't care,

because he loves me."

"'*Because he loves me*,'" Leo mocked. "'Cause your life's a fucking fairy tale, ain't it?"

Charlie scowled and looked like he wanted to be a dick right back, but he didn't. He said nothing and went back to his work, and the silence stung. Leo could handle a row, or a punch up, but the guilt in his gut at hurting Charlie's feelings bothered him more than he cared to admit.

"Where does 'de Sousa' come from? Is it Spanish or something?"

For a long moment, Leo feared Charlie wouldn't answer, then he set his pencil down and picked up another. "It's Brazilian," he said. "I was born in São Paulo."

"São Paulo?"

"Yup. Got dumped in an orphanage when I was a baby."

Wow. Leo had figured Fliss and Charlie had to have come from shitty backgrounds to end up in foster care, but he'd imagined something closer to home. "Do you remember it?"

Charlie finally looked Leo's way. "Nope. My first memory is drawing on my bedroom wall with one of Kate's lipsticks."

The art teacher cut off Leo's reply by tapping Leo's closed sketchbook. "Make a start please, Mr. Hendry. I want to see an outline by the end of the lesson." Leo glanced up, irritated. The teacher smiled and held out a pencil. "Come on. If I don't see some lines, I'll have to find you a seat at the front."

At the front? Stuff that too. Leo liked people where he could see them. He opened the book and considered the view through the window. Neither option Charlie had mentioned seemed worth a punt, and Leo hadn't put a pencil to paper in . . . shit, he couldn't even remember. Not that he'd ever been particularly good at it.

Why the hell did I take art again?

He had no idea. Choosing his GCSE options at the end of

year nine seemed so long ago—

Charlie nudged him. "Just draw something, will you? You'll be in enough trouble as it is, if Mrs. Parkin reports you."

"What do you care?"

"Fine. I don't care. Do what you want and end up a loser like Wayne bloody Murphy."

"Who?"

"Enough." The art teacher had come back. "Charlie, set a good example, please. I expect better of you."

The reprimand went over Leo's head, but Charlie frowned, clearly rattled. He hunched over his work, blocking Leo, and didn't speak again for the rest of the lesson.

Leo entertained himself by sketching the waist-length French plait of the girl in front of him. When that was done, he slumped forward on the table, pillowed his head on his good arm, and took in his classmates—the girls first, all nine of them. A blonde across the room shot him a shy smile. Leo rolled his eyes and looked away. Attention from girls came easy. Shame he didn't want it.

He turned his consideration to the boys—just four in total, minus Charlie—two blonds, a redhead, and a boy with such short hair it was hard to tell the colour. None of them held Leo's interest. Not like Charlie.

Charlie, Charlie, Charlie.

His leg was so close, Leo felt his body heat everywhere, and considered what it would feel like for real, if their legs actually touched, even with the barrier of their school trousers.

Fuck.

Leo sat up and forced himself to shift away from Charlie. Across the room, the blonde girl was glancing his way again, except she wasn't looking at Leo, she was looking at Charlie, and Charlie was grinning right back. An odd pain flared in Leo's veins. He'd never seen Charlie smile like that, eyes shining, teeth pure white against his tanned skin. Why hadn't he seen Charlie smile like that?

'Cause you've only known him a week, douche bag.

The bell rang for the end of the lesson. The classroom burst into life, stools scraping the floor, bags hitting the benches. Leo stretched his good arm over his head. Despite his preoccupation with Charlie's smile, he'd half dozed off. He stuffed his sketchbook into his bag and watched Charlie do the same with a little more care. "What lesson do you have next?"

Charlie shot Leo a surprised glance. "Double maths with Mr. Rogers. Same as you."

"How do you know what lesson I have?"

"Reg asked the school to give me your timetable, in case you got lost or forgot—"

"Yeah, yeah." Leo got the picture. Bloody Reg. He'd been like a rash since Leo had puked on his shoes in the doctor's surgery. Like half carrying him to the car and putting him to bed had meant something. It hadn't, save the fact that Leo was too much of a pussy to face his own skin. "I'm not going to get lost."

"Whatever." Charlie fished a packet of chewing gum out of his bag and handed them to Leo. "If you're gonna smoke on the way home, use these. Mum can smell fags a mile off."

It was on the tip of Leo's tongue to say that he didn't give a witch's tit if Kate knew he smoked, but he was fast discovering that being a twat to Charlie was no fun. Instead he followed Charlie out of the classroom and into a bustling corridor. Students barged and shoved. A sports bag hit Leo's bandaged arm, and he grunted. The scar tissue was already sore from his adventure over the fence. He wanted to rub it, but pride stopped him. No one here knew that he was half human, half burned-up zombie.

They were halfway across the quad when Leo saw the blood dripping down his hand.

SIX

Charlie pushed open the door to the maths block. Bloody Leo. Reg had said from the start that school was a bad idea for him, and Charlie, though he'd quietly fought in Leo's corner, was beginning to believe he'd been right. Wayne feckin' Murphy. Seriously? *Nice one, Leo. Why don't you buddy up with the skanky stoners behind the library while you're at it?*

The thought made Charlie shudder. He'd smelt weed on Leo a few nights ago, he was sure of it . . . almost. The other side of his brain was convinced he'd dreamed it. He'd woken every night in the past week, consumed by a compulsive need to check on Leo, only to find Lila already with him, and Leo wouldn't smoke weed with her in the room, right?

Of course he wouldn't. Leo's weird moods gave Charlie whiplash, but no one could doubt his affection for Lila.

"Charlie."

"*What?*" Charlie stopped walking and turned around. Leo had hardly spoken in days, but it felt like he wouldn't shut up today. Then he found Leo right behind him, clutching his left arm to his chest. Charlie frowned. Leo's left arm was the one he wore a bandage on. "What's the matter?"

Silence. For a moment, Charlie thought he'd imagined Leo calling his name, and then he noticed Leo's wide eyes and ashen skin, his teeth biting into his bottom lip, and the thin line of blood trickling down his left hand. *Shit.* Charlie's stomach churned. "Have you cut yourself?"

Leo shook his head. He looked like he might be sick too. "I need to get out of here."

"'Out of here'? Do you need to see the nurse?"

"No, I need to *go.*"

Leo started to back up. Charlie caught his good arm. "Go where? Are you going home?"

In answer, Leo wrenched himself free and turned away. He was by the door before Charlie caught up and grabbed him again.

"Wait. I'll come with you." The words were out before he could stop them, even though he knew Leo intended to escape far more than the bustling corridors. Knew Leo was about to lead him down a path he'd never thought to travel. "Come on. I know somewhere we can go."

He ducked out of the maths block without waiting for Leo's response and led the way to the sports pavilion, and snuck round the back. There was a gap in the trees behind the old wooden building that took them to a disused railway track by the canal. He picked a path through the bushes until they came to the bridge. "Come on," he said. "We can sit by the water."

"Under the bridge?"

It was the first time Leo had spoken since they'd left school grounds. His voice was hoarse and tired, and Charlie slowed to let him catch up. "Yeah. All the bunkers used to come here before the council built the bandstand in the park."

"You never did, though, did you?"

"What do you think?"

Leo made a sound that could've been a snort of laughter, but there was no humour in his face as they came to the sacred spot beneath the bridge—dark, sheltered, and covered with graffiti.

Charlie dropped his bag and sat down by the water, leaning back on the blacked-out bricks of the bridge. Leo hesitated a moment before he did the same.

"You're going to get in trouble for this," he said.

Charlie waved his concern away. "Doubt it. Rogers is a dozy idiot. He wouldn't notice if the whole class didn't show up, and even if he does, I reckon we can blag our way out of it."

"Yeah?" Leo unzipped his coat and slipped his good arm out of its sleeve. "What are you gonna say?"

"Dunno. That you were tired or something, probably. It is your first day and all."

Leo said nothing. Was he regretting his decision to come to school?

"Are you going to sort your arm out?"

"Hmm?"

"Your arm," Charlie repeated. "It's still bleeding."

Leo looked down at his arm and slowly began to peel away his coat sleeve. His school jumper came next, then his shirt sleeve and bandage, both stained an ominous red.

Charlie swallowed hard, but the sight of Leo's blood was just the start. *Oh God, his arm.* From his elbow to his shoulder, Leo's arm was utterly ruined, a marbled mess of scarred flesh . . . burned flesh.

Leo's flesh.

His body.

His skin.

Leo.

"Stop fucking staring."

Charlie jumped. "I'm not."

"Bollocks, you aren't." Leo snorted. "Do you think I don't get enough of that? Bloody doctors poking and prodding me."

"I'm not staring," Charlie insisted, though he had been. "And I'm not prodding you, am I? I'm over here."

"Whatever."

Leo's voice had lost its fire. He shifted and angled his body away while he did something to his arm, shoulders hunched, head bowed. Even with his diminished view, Charlie could tell it hurt. He let Leo be awhile and considered the dingy spot Charlie had picked to hide out in. Dank, dark, and littered with rubbish, it was hardly the best place for first aid. Still, Charlie had observed Leo enough to reckon it was this or nothing.

Leo hissed, pained and low. Charlie chanced a hand on his other arm. "Is it really messed up?"

"Dunno. It's so bloody I can't see."

Charlie steeled himself and clambered over Leo's legs to crouch by the water. His stomach churned. Leo was right: in his elbow joint, there was nothing to see but a smeared mess of blood. "We should clean it."

"We?"

Charlie ignored Leo and stretched for his bag. Inside he found the bottle of mineral water Kate insisted everyone left the house with each day, and popped the sports cap. He tipped it over Leo's arm. It helped a little, but not enough, so he looked around for something to wipe it with. Nothing seemed suitable. *Stuff it.* He tore a strip off his own shirt.

Leo's eyes widened. "What are you doing?"

"Cleaning you up." Charlie soaked the scrap of fabric in water, held Leo's arm still, and laid the wet fabric over Leo's elbow joint, covering the worst of the blood.

Leo winced.

"Am I hurting you?" Charlie asked.

"No." But Leo's shiver said otherwise.

Charlie took his hands from Leo and tore another strip from his shirt to dry Leo's arm with. "Are you all right?"

Leo nodded. "Yeah, sorry. It's just seeing it . . . makes me . . . you know?"

Charlie filled in the blanks. Oddly, the more he stared at Leo's mangled flesh, the less it bothered him, but the blood? He shuddered, glad that most of it was hidden by the scraps of his shirt. "Do you feel sick?"

"I do now."

"Eh?"

"Hold my wrist again, will ya?"

"Erm, okay." Charlie took Leo's injured arm and gripped his wrist, loosely at first until Leo's stare seemed to compel him to squeeze tighter and press his thumb into the pulse point thrumming beneath Leo's warm skin.

Leo closed his eyes. His head dropped. "Your hands are cold."

"Sorry."

"Nah." Leo shook his head. "It's good."

He didn't say anything more for a long while. Charlie entertained himself by clearing the last of the blood from Leo's arm and inspecting the new damage. Despite the mess, he couldn't see much, save a small tear in Leo's elbow crease. Charlie was no expert, but it didn't appear particularly deep, especially compared to the original wound. He stared at the mottled mass of scars and skin and pondered the horror behind it. There'd been a fire, he knew that, because Lila's lungs were damaged from the smoke, but what on earth had happened to Leo?

By the time three o'clock rolled around, Charlie's imagination had left him no wiser. He roused Leo with a gentle nudge. "We need to chip. I've got to get my bike from school."

Leo raised his head and treated Charlie to a bleary gaze. "Where are we going?"

"Home," Charlie said. "School's nearly over. We can't stay here all night."

Leo looked as though he wanted to do just that, but he got to his feet anyway and rolled his sleeves down. He didn't appear to notice that his arm was now clean. "How are you going to get your bike? What if a teacher sees you?"

Charlie snorted. "I might be a nerd, but Andy and Fliss went through that school before me, and they taught me every escape route going. Trust me, I won't be seen."

And he wasn't. He left Leo on the canal path, slipped around the back of the food tech block, and retrieved his BMX. When he got back, he half expected Leo to be gone, but he was there, hands in his pockets, head down, and apparently in a world of his own.

They made their way home. Charlie kept a sharp eye out for Darren Stroud and his gang, but there was no sign of them, which was odd, but Leo's silence distracted Charlie from pondering it much.

Charlie glanced at him and felt a little strange. He'd never bunked off school before, and though he reckoned it was unlikely either of them would be missed, nerves still gnawed at his gut. Kate often saw right through him. She'd know the second they got home, he was sure of it.

Sure of it, and wrong. Kate greeted them both with an absent smile, caught up in a game of Uno with Lila. It was a while before she remembered it had been Leo's first day at school and said she was going to check on him, and by then Charlie's shirt was loitering at the bottom of the recycling bin, and Leo was fast asleep, fully clothed—coat and all—on his bed.

Kate came downstairs from checking on him. "How was today, Charlie? Is Leo feeling poorly again? He's out like a light."

Charlie shrugged. He'd never got to the bottom of what had been wrong with Leo the week before, and he couldn't think how to explain what had happened under the bridge without incriminating them both.

Kate took a seat at the table and peered at the history homework Charlie had spent most of the afternoon staring at. "Hitler, eh? I liked studying Stalin better. We have a book somewhere about the siege of Leningrad. *City of Thieves*, I think. I'll ask Reg."

Charlie rolled his eyes. Kate and Reg were both bookworms —the house was full of them—but Charlie didn't much care for reading. Comics aside, why read when he'd rather draw? "No, thanks."

"I'll dig it out anyway. You might change your mind. In the meantime, you can tell me what Leo did to his arm today."

Busted. Charlie's heart skipped like the tick of a broken clock. "What do you mean?"

"I'm putting my mother instinct together with the blood on his coat sleeve, and combining it with the shifty look you've had since you came home. Spit it out, Charlie. Whatever it is, I won't be cross."

Charlie believed that, for the most part, but he wasn't so sure about Leo. Their time under the bridge had been spent mostly in silence, and grassing Leo up felt like an act of betrayal.

He considered his options while Kate waited, tapping her fingers on the table. A half-truth seemed the only way. "I think he pulled it a bit at lunchtime. I helped him clean it up. It wasn't too bad."

"Did he see the nurse?"

"He didn't want to."

And you walked home together?"

Charlie nodded. "Yeah. He was fine, just a bit tired."

Kate appeared satisfied, for now at least. She left Charlie to it and got on with dinner, and when Leo appeared in time to inhale his supper and bath Lila, she made no comment, save a casual enquiry about his first day at Heyton High.

Leo didn't come back downstairs after he'd put Lila to bed. Charlie let him be. Leo kept to himself most nights, unless Kate or Reg asked him to stay with the family.

Around ten, Fliss came home from work and summoned Charlie to the attic.

"What do you want?" Charlie hovered warily by the ladder. He wasn't often granted access to Fliss's lair.

"You need to tell Leo to stop flicking his spliff butts onto the garage roof. Dad's going up there at the weekend to clean the guttering, and there's going to be too many to blame it on next door."

"Why do I need to tell him? Tell him yourself."

Fliss rolled her eyes. "When am I supposed to do that? At the dinner table? Or when he's bathing Lila? I hardly ever see him, numpty."

Lucky Leo, though to be fair, Charlie didn't see much of Fliss either. "Why are you assuming it's him?"

"Who else would it be? You've never had so much as a drag on a smoke, have you?"

She said it like it was a bad thing, but Charlie ignored that. Andy and Fliss had both told him over and over that they'd kick the shit out of him if they ever caught him smoking. Not that it was likely to happen. He'd never seen the attraction in lacing his lungs with tar. "How do you know they're joints?"

"Please." Fliss threw herself into her computer chair and flicked the monitor to life. "I smelt weed on him the day he got here, not that I give a shit what he does. I just don't want the hassle of Mum and Dad getting all CIA on us again, like they were when Jason stole that Valium from Mrs. Oliver."

Charlie remembered Jason. He'd stayed with them for three

months a few years ago, but in that time had wreaked more havoc than anyone had been quite able to believe. The last straw had been when he'd burgled the elderly neighbours across the street. Kate and Reg had vowed not to take another teenager after that . . . until Leo. "Leo's not like Jason."

Fliss tossed a distracted glance at Charlie, clearly already engrossed in whatever crap kept her occupied on the internet. "I know that. Leo's a nice kid. Fucked up, but nice. Which is why you need to stop him getting himself kicked out. Now piss off. I've got shit to do."

Charlie took his dismissal and swung himself out of the loft. He showered and then slipped into his bedroom, automatically checking on Leo on his way past.

Leo was asleep again, lights on, curtains open. With a sigh, Charlie swapped the main light for his own lamp that had somehow appeared in Leo's room, but left the curtains open. He left the door ajar too. Lila didn't crawl into Leo's bed every night, but Charlie had got into the habit of making things easier for her not to wake Leo when she did—leaving the landing light on, and clearing the floor of clutter.

He hadn't long been in bed when Reg came knocking at his door. Charlie glanced up from his sketchpad in surprise. It was usually Kate who paid him bedtime visits. "Hey, Dad. What's up?"

"I was hoping that you would tell me."

"Huh?"

Reg's frown deepened, and he sat on the end of Charlie's bed. "I've had an email from the school this evening. Apparently you and Leo were disruptive in your art class, and then you were missing all afternoon. And this was after Leo was caught leaving the premises at lunchtime. I hope you have a good explanation, young man, because I am *very* disappointed in you right now."

Charlie gulped. Reg's disappointment was awful and hung around the house like a grey cloud until the offender did something to make him proud again. "Um—"

Reg held up his hand. "And don't even think about feeding me the story you did your mother earlier. Telling fibs like that was extremely irresponsible, Charlie. You know how important it is that we know what's going on with Leo. Why did you lie?"

"I didn't lie."

"But you were economical with the truth?"

Charlie couldn't deny it. "I didn't tell Mum about lunchtime because I didn't want to get Leo in trouble. And I brought him home early because he was upset and he'd hurt his arm."

"You didn't come home early. Mum said you were on time. Where were you all afternoon?"

"Under the bridge. Leo was upset, and I helped him wash his arm. Dad, he wouldn't have let anyone else do it—you *know* that—and I didn't want him to go off on his own."

Reg said nothing for a long moment, his pale gaze as inscrutable as it always was when Charlie was in trouble, and then he sighed, weary and deep, and Charlie felt almost as bad for him as he had for Leo. "All right, son. Thank you for telling me the truth. I appreciate that, but you have to know how serious this is, okay? One of the conditions of us taking Leo was that he had to settle into school as quickly as possible. Mum and I can handle whatever he throws our way, but we can't tolerate any disruption to your education. Do you understand what I'm saying?"

"You're saying that you'll send him away," Charlie said sullenly.

"It would be an absolute last resort, son, but we'd do it if his behaviour had a detrimental effect on you. Is that clear?"

"Yes." There was nothing else Charlie could say. Mum and

Dad hated sending kids away, but he had no doubt that they'd do it to protect the family they already had. "Um, Dad?"

"Yes?"

"Are you going to tell Leo I told you about him being upset?"

Reg's stern expression wilted briefly, and he shook his head. "No. I'm going to tell him what the school told me in the email, and then give him the same warning I've given you. It's only fair that he knows where he stands, Charlie. We can't give him everything, but we can give him that."

With one last pointed frown, Reg left the room. Despite the anxious disquiet in Charlie's belly, sleep came quickly, the darkness closing in like a warm blanket, and it was the early hours of the morning before Leo's distress woke him.

He shot upright, his heart in his mouth. He'd grown used to Leo's nighttime muttering—they both slept with their doors open—and Lila's wandering, but tonight, like the very first night, Leo's low cry cut Charlie to the bone.

He scrambled out of bed, crossed the landing, and dashed into Leo's room, catching him as he began to flail. "Shh, Leo. It's okay."

Leo's eyes snapped open. He met Charlie's gaze for a brief, heart-stopping second before his expression grew vacant and he was lost again. Charlie crouched by the bed, hand wrapped tight around Leo's wrist. He pressed his thumb into the pulse point and counted Leo's racing heartbeat. "Come on, Leo. Wake up if it's too bad. It's not real, I promise."

But as he whispered the words, Charlie's eyes were drawn up Leo's arm to the fresh bandage, and suddenly his mind was filled with an image of mangled skin and blood . . . of flames, smoke, and smouldering flesh. Leo's flesh.

Charlie's knees went weak. He fell back, still gripping Leo's wrist, and pressed his face into his knees. *"It's not real, I promise."* What a load of bollocks. Of course it was real . . . real to Leo, and trapped in his sleep, scarred and alone, he'd never be free of it.

SEVEN

Andy Poulton eased his car into a parking space. "You look more impressed than Charlie did when I brought him last year."

I'll say. Wembley. Bloody hell. Leo gazed around. He'd been on a school trip to Swindon Town FC once, but he'd never seen anything like the *huge* national stadium. It almost took away the discomfort of being stuck in a car with Reg's eldest son.

Almost, though oddly enough, despite his imposing size, Andy didn't seem to trigger the monster in Leo's belly—the one that made his palms sweat and his lips go numb. Perhaps Andy was playing nice, because, so far, Leo had somehow managed to behave like a normal person.

"Charlie doesn't like football," Leo said to fill the awkward silence that Andy didn't seem to have noticed.

Andy snorted. "Ain't that the truth. I dragged him kicking and screaming to a Champions League game last year. Little twerp fell asleep."

The image made Leo feel like smiling, but an unwelcome recollection dampened his humour: a few nights' old hazy memory of waking to find Charlie asleep on the bedroom floor, curled up far closer to Leo's bed than he ever ventured when Leo was awake.

They got out of the car and made their way into the stadium.

"So, who are you supporting?" Andy asked. "Arsenal or City?"

"Hmm?" Leo glanced at Andy's red football shirt. "Better be the Gunners, hadn't it? If we're sitting at their end and all."

Andy shrugged like it didn't matter, and as they found their seats, Leo kind of agreed. A year ago, he'd have given anything to be at a Premiership game like this, dreamed of it, but now the building roar of the crowd felt like it was drawing the breath from his lungs.

He sat down in the plastic seat Andy directed him to and thought of Charlie again. Thought of his shrewd, kind eyes, and the smooth brown skin of his back . . . the back Leo seemed to open his eyes to every morning as Charlie got dressed in plain sight of the reflection in Leo's window. His pulse quickened. Damn. Thinking of Charlie was usually as good as the doctor's fuzzy pills. It calmed Leo down. Helped him sleep. But Charlie's back—

"So how are you settling in at Casa Poulton?"

Leo jumped. He hadn't noticed Andy dropping into the seat beside him, which was odd, because the bloke was massive. "'Casa Poulton'?"

"Yeah, Ma and Pa's, like. Getting on okay?"

"Fine." Leo shrugged and fixed his gaze on the giant screen at the Gunners' end of the pitch. He'd been asked that question a lot recently—by teachers, doctors, social workers—and his answer was always the same, because it was the answer they wanted to hear, the answer that meant they could go on their way, convinced they'd filled their quota of good deeds. Not that Reg seemed particularly satisfied with how his latest project was panning out. *"We won't tolerate any disruption to Charlie . . ."*

Yeah, yeah. Like Leo had asked him to bunk off school. *Glad he did, though, aren't you?*

Leo shuddered, his arm tingling as he recalled Charlie cleaning it, trying to soothe the burn with far more than the cool water. Charlie was good, not like Leo. And Reg clearly knew it too.

Andy nudged Leo. "You there, mate?"

"Huh?"

Andy grinned. "Away with the bloody fairies. You teenagers are all the same. I was saying that it isn't anything to be ashamed of to find it tough to settle down. I've seen enough of you kids go through that house to know it takes time. What's it been, a month? Two? I reckon you've got a ways to go yet."

Wanker. But Leo couldn't deny it. In the month they'd been in Heyton, Lila had become more settled with every day that passed, creeping into Leo's bed less and less, but Leo? Not even close.

His pocket vibrated. He pulled out the phone Kate had given him last weekend, and on the screen was a text from Reg: *Lila bathed and ready for bed. Reading Goldilocks with Kate.*

Leo scowled. This was Reg's latest trick since he'd come to Leo's room and given him his first strike—using Lila to get to him. *Bastard.*

"So," Andy said, reminding Leo that he hadn't answered him. "How's it all going? Has Fliss thrown her biker boots at your head yet?"

Leo sniggered before he caught himself. "Not me. She chucked olive oil at Charlie last night, though."

"Sounds about right." Andy craned his neck as the emcee announced the players to the pitch. "Don't be scared of her though. Her bark's worse than her bite."

"I'm not scared of Fliss." How could Leo be when she was so kind to Lila? If Kate was out when Leo left for school, he always took Lila to Fliss's room. "She's nice."

Andy shot him a disbelieving stare. "How have you worked that out so quick? Takes most folk years to see through that chip on her shoulder."

Leo shrugged. "She's good to Lila and me."

"She's a great girl," Andy agreed. "She just doesn't want anyone to know it. Bloody hell, look . . . it's about to start."

Leo followed Andy's gaze to the pitch and saw the teams were in position with the referee about to blow his whistle. The biggest football match he'd probably ever see was about to kick off and . . . he didn't care. *It's like I'm dead inside.* And if it weren't for the tremor in his hands, and the sweat dripping down his back, he'd have thought he was.

The game passed in a blur of flashing lights and suffocating noise. Andy bought Leo a pasty at halftime, but Leo hid it under his seat. Recently, Kate's shepherd's pie was the only thing that didn't burn a hole in his belly and make him feel like he'd swallowed a bottle of acid.

Out of nowhere, Andy thumped Leo's back. "Three nil. Good game, eh? Did you see van Persie's goal? That's gonna be on Match of the Day, for sure."

Leo nodded and tried to find a response coherent enough to satisfy the eager grin on Andy's face, because despite being obviously Team Reg, he was proving hard to hate. "Yeah, it was good."

Andy shook his head. "'Good'? Bloody teenagers. What's happened to you all? My mum couldn't shut me up when I was your age. Come on. Let's fight our way back to the car."

And a fight it was. The exit routes were crammed with chanting fans, shoulder to shoulder, elbows jostling with every step. Leo feared he might puke, until Andy got behind him and caged him within his massive arms.

Outside, fresh air hit Leo like a truck. He bent double and sucked it in until his chest ached from the effort. Andy squeezed his shoulder. His touch wasn't magic like Charlie's, but Leo felt no urge to shake him off.

"Better?" Andy asked. "Can get a little stuffy in there, can't it?"

Leo nodded. He wanted a smoke, and was sure he'd smelt tobacco on Andy earlier, but common sense told him that asking for a fag would be more trouble than it was worth. "What are we doing now?"

"Going home, via McDonald's, if that's all right with you. I'm bloody starved."

Leo didn't see how, given the huge pie and chips Andy had put away during the match, but he shrugged. Despite missing Charlie's quiet presence, he had no desire to return to the house anytime soon. Nights there were long and dark, even with the lamp he'd pinched from Charlie's room. "Okay."

Andy drove them out of London and stopped at a service station on the M25. McDonald's was closed for refurbishment, so he parked up at KFC, went inside, and came back with enough chicken to feed a small army.

Leo picked at his food, relieved Andy hadn't made him go into the restaurant, and a comfortable silence enveloped them.

Comfortable?

Really?

Leo turned the word over in his mind, testing it, but it fit. The only other time he could recall the feeling recently was when he'd played Xbox in the cellar with Charlie—quiet evenings spent side by side on the battered sofa bed, shoulder to shoulder, battling it out with zombies and flamethrowers.

"I was thinking of taking Lila to Legoland next weekend. Do you think she'd like that?"

Leo glanced up at Andy. "Lila? Why? What's she to you?"

"My little sister, for the time being." Andy fixed Leo with a steady gaze. "Listen, I know it's taken a while for me to take you out, but that's only because social services muck about so much with their paperwork. If I'd had my way, we'd have done this weeks ago."

"What's it got to do with social services?"

"I needed to be approved before I was allowed to drive you and Lila around, be alone with you, stuff like that. You know the rules." Leo was mystified. Andy frowned, then something seemed to click. "Shit, I keep forgetting you're not one of those kids who's been in the system for years. This is all new to you, eh?"

"I don't know what the fuck you're talking about."

Andy shrugged. "Hopefully, you'll never need to. Okay, let me put it like this: Dad and Kate have been taking kids like you for as long as I can remember, but it's something we *all* do really, as a family. So the way I see it, I've got two extra siblings to take care of for a while."

"'Take care of'?"

"Yep. I'm your big brother, like it or not, and for you that means football, bowling, and, 'cause you're a teenager and shit, the occasional sneaky pint. Just don't tell Ma."

Leo didn't know what to say. A sneaky pint sounded awesome, but the rest of it? The bloke was taking the piss. He had to be, right? "Did you take Charlie out when he was Lila's age?"

"Sometimes, not to the football, though. He's always been a nerd, so we spent a lot of time at the cinema, in silence, 'cause the little squirt didn't talk until he was about eight."

Leo tied a knot in an extra-long chip and rubbed the oozing grease between his fingers. "He didn't talk?"

"Nope. Never said a word. They reckoned he'd been taught to be quiet at the orphanage. Seen and not heard, maybe? Didn't stop him crying all night when he was a baby, though."

Leo's chest hurt. He couldn't picture Charlie as a toddler, alone and unwanted on the other side of the world. It didn't make any sense. Who in their right mind wouldn't want Charlie?

I want Charlie.

Later that night, Leo let himself into the silent Poulton house. He checked on Lila, then took a shower and redressed his arm. The small tear he'd sustained from vaulting the school fence had healed, and he could look at it now without retching.

Didn't stop him pulling a hoodie over his T-shirt, though. Hiding the bandage meant he could pretend it wasn't there until morning came and it was time to face it all over again.

On his way back to his bedroom, he peeked through Charlie's open door and found Charlie asleep, facedown on a sketchpad, still clutching a pen. Leo wondered absently what he'd been drawing, but Charlie's cheek obscured the page.

Leo crept into the room and pried the pen from Charlie's slack fingers. He set it on the bedside table, then hovered, suddenly transfixed by Charlie's slender wrist.

I want to hold it.

The notion made Leo's head swim, and he let the thought grow and morph into a vision of him reaching out and closing his hand around Charlie's arm, feeling the warmth of his skin and the steady beat of his pulse. Then he pictured sliding his fingers lower to twine with Charlie's, because Charlie's hands were magic. Leo felt them on him every time he closed his eyes. Every time darkness flickered in his fractured subconscious and threatened to pull him under. Charlie had touched him that way only once—or twice, maybe; Leo wasn't sure—but even long after Charlie had let him go, Leo's skin had smouldered with the best kind of heat. A heat that healed every hurt Leo had ever known.

Would it feel like that for Charlie? If Leo touched him too? *Would it fuck.*

Leo retreated to his own room and crawled into bed. The room swallowed him up, but with the curtains half open and the lamp glowing its soft light, he didn't feel as suffocated as he sometimes did. Didn't feel the need to knock on Kate's door for a pill to help him drift. Instead he closed his eyes and pictured Charlie asleep, imagined the rise and fall of his chest, and the flutter of his eyelids as he dreamed.

EIGHT

A week later, Charlie pulled on a clean T-shirt, hyperaware—as he'd become every time they were in the same room—of Leo watching him.

"Are you going out?" Leo asked.

His tone suggested he didn't care much for the answer, so Charlie shrugged and rummaged in a drawer for a hoodie to ward off the stiff breeze rattling the windows.

"Where are you going?"

Charlie glanced around. Leo was on Charlie's bed, stretched out, his good arm behind his head. *See? He doesn't give a crap.* But Charlie paused anyway. Leo had a way of staring at him that made him forget what he was doing. Made him forget everything except the vortex of his stormy gaze. "I'm meeting Jess and Lucy at the park."

"The wicked witches?"

Charlie rolled his eyes. Despite Jess's and Lucy's best efforts to befriend Leo, he'd ignored them as much as he seemed to ignore everyone that wasn't Charlie or Wayne knobhead Murphy. "You've met the rest of the girls in our year, mate. *They're* the bloody witches."

Leo scowled—like he always did when Charlie forgot himself and called him *mate*—but Charlie couldn't be arsed to placate him. It had been a long week, and Leo's moods had begun to grate on him. *Is it really so hard to be civil?*

"Anyway." Charlie stamped into his scuffed Converse and drifted to the open door. "I'll see you later, yeah?"

"Whatever."

Leo rolled off the bed and squeezed around Charlie. Their shoulders brushed, their legs, their hands, and Charlie shuddered, a barely there tremble that tickled his nerves. Leo glanced back. Did he feel it too? By his blank stare, probably not, but then the apathy melted from Leo's face and he let loose one of his elusive grins.

"Can I come to the park with you?"

They walked into town in near silence. Leo wasn't much of a talker, and Charlie was still reeling from the scene in the bedroom—that imagined encounter that made him feel warm all over. Damn Leo and his hypnotic eyes. *Why does he have to look at me like that?*

For all he knew, Leo looked at *everyone* like that, but that oddly painful notion did nothing to calm the roiling in his belly.

"So, what do you do in the parks around here on a Friday night? Back home, we get stoned and break stuff."

Charlie chanced a glance at Leo. He rarely mentioned the life he must've had before him and Lila came to Heyton, and he'd never referred to Swindon as *home* before. In fact, Charlie reckoned he'd never heard Leo use the word at all. "Um, some of the girls smoke puff. I'd rather have beer, though. Smoking's for skanks."

Leo took the dig with the insolent smirk that drove Charlie

crazy in so many conflicting ways. "Where do you get beer from? Do you nick it from Reg?"

"What? No! House rules mean no stealing, remember? Fuck that. We buy it from the SPAR shop. Jess's sister works in there. Can't tonight, though. Haven't got any money."

"I've got a tenner." Leo pulled out a Velcro wallet Charlie hadn't seen before.

"Arsenal? Where'd you get that?"

"Andy gave it to me."

Ah. That made sense. Leo still avoided Reg like the plague, but he didn't seem to mind Andy.

"Come on, then," Leo said. "Let's get some cans."

Turned out Leo's idea of cans was the biggest bottle of cheap rum they could find. Bev, Jess's sister, eyed them dubiously as Leo handed over his crumpled tenner, and Charlie couldn't blame her. *Rum? Really?* He didn't know about Leo, but he had a feeling that two swigs from that ominous-looking bottle would have him puking in the bushes with the WKD girls from Old Farm Park. *And what about Leo?*

Charlie swallowed thickly. Hard-core drinking was probably on the list of sins that could get Leo sent away. "Are you sure you want that?" he asked when they were back on the street, the bottle safely hidden in Leo's coat.

"It's booze, innit?" Leo's tone was playful, but when he met Charlie's gaze, his eyes had dulled, like they often did when Reg tried to engage him. "Fuck this shit. I wanna get smashed."

Despite the unease prickling his neck, Charlie knew better than to argue, and they walked the rest of the way to the park in silence, side by side, arms swinging just a hairsbreadth away from each other. At the park entrance, an icy wind whistled through the trees. Charlie shivered. Leo glanced at him. "Cold?"

"Nope." Charlie shoved his hands in his pockets. "Come on. The girls are waiting by the splash park."

Leo snorted. "Bloody girls."

"Suit yourself. Stoners hang under the bandstand."

Charlie set off across the muddy football pitch. He figured Leo would drift away to find Wayne and his gang of twats, so a hand on his arm caught him off guard a few moments later.

"Which girls are you meeting again? Jess and Lucy?"

"You really give a shit?"

Leo shrugged. "Not particularly. I don't like girls."

Charlie tripped over his own feet. "You don't like girls?"

"They're annoying, all that fucking staring and cackling. Don't know how you spend so much time with them."

Because it's easier than pretending to be one of the boys. "I grew up with Fliss, remember? No one's as annoying as her."

Leo's reply was cut off by a shout from somewhere in the darkness. Charlie stared in the direction it had come from as three figures emerged from the gloom. Jess, Lucy, and Lucy's cousin Meg surrounded them, grinning at Charlie and eyeing Leo with a speculative interest that reminded Charlie of a gang of feral cats he'd once seen on holiday.

He kicked Jess and shot her a meaningful glare. "All right?"

Jess's grin widened as she artfully avoided his gaze. "And then some. Hi, Leo."

Leo grunted and pulled a packet of cigarettes from his coat pocket.

If Jess was bothered by Leo's flat response, she didn't show it. Instead, she winked and threaded her arm through Charlie's. "Come on. Let's go find Maria. She's got some vodka."

Charlie suppressed a sigh. Vodka, rum, weed—apparently however the night panned out, he'd be carrying someone home.

An hour or so later, his money was on Lucy, who was

slumped against him, giggling at whatever Jess was mouthing to her behind her hand. *Daft twats.*

Charlie sighed and tuned them out, scanning the dark park, squinting at the scattered groups huddled on the grass, illuminated by the glow of phone screens and whatever they were smoking. Wayne Murphy's group usually hung around by the basketball court, but Charlie couldn't see that far, let alone tell if Leo—who'd long since grown bored with the girls and wandered off—was with them.

"Earth to Charlie?" Lucy waved her hand in front of his face. "What are you staring at?"

"Hmm? Oh, nothing."

Lucy lost interest fast, but Charlie's fixation with the most distant hooded group remained. His gaze fell on a figure at the edge, the only one not holding a phone. Leo had one, but his solitary ways meant he rarely used it.

Agitation burned in Charlie's veins. Suddenly, he had to be sure the lonely figure was Leo.

He scrambled to his feet. The girls, preoccupied with their vodka, paid him no heed until he stepped over them.

Jess caught his arm. "Where are you going?"

Charlie shook her off. "To find Leo. He, um, has my house key."

It was a plausible explanation. She let him go, and he set off across the park. As he got closer to the group by the basketball court, the wind picked up again. He shivered, wishing he'd worn his other jacket, and pulled his hood up, smirking at the irony. *I'll fit right in over there.*

"Charlie?"

Charlie jumped and whirled around. Leo was behind him, half-empty rum bottle in one hand, a fat joint in the other. "Okay?"

Leo raised an eyebrow. "Was gonna ask you the same thing. You look like you're on your way to off someone."

"Seriously?"

"Why not?" Leo shrugged and offered a lopsided grin that suggested he was probably as trashed as he'd planned. "You're dressed all black and shit. Like an assassin."

"Don't know what assassins you've ever seen. And my shoes are blue."

Leo snorted. "Like I can even see them. Dark, innit?"

Charlie let it go. He'd spent most of the evening talking in circles with pissed-up girls. He couldn't be arsed to do it with Leo. "What are you doing on your own? Thought you'd be over there with the knobheads."

"Knobheads? You mean Wayne? You're a bit of a twat about him, you know. He's sound."

It was Charlie's turn to snort. "You only think that because he gives you weed."

"Howd'ya know that?"

"Because Reg doesn't give you enough money to buy your own."

Leo fixed Charlie with a sphinx-like stare. "I meant how do you know I smoke weed, but I guess the bifta in my hand gives me away, eh?"

"A little." Charlie chanced a grin. "And Fliss told me too. Nothing gets past her."

"So she keeps telling me. Anyway, what are you doing, bowling across the park? I thought *you'd* be living it up with your gang of birds."

"Got bored. Thought I'd come and find you."

"Why?"

"Why not? Live in the same house, don't we?" Charlie shifted his weight from one foot to the other. Leo had a way of making him feel like the biggest idiot in the world. He'd set off to find him with no plans for what he'd say when he did, and he had an inkling Leo somehow knew it. "Um, anyway. I should probably get back."

Leo moved close enough for Charlie to smell the rum on his breath. "Fuck that. Let's go for a walk."

Charlie trailed Leo to the disused railway line that ran parallel to the far side of the park. Leo didn't say much, but then he rarely did. They climbed over the wooden gate, and Leo gazed around and took a seat on an old bench. "This place is messed up."

"Nah, it's just old. Haven't been any trains through here since the seventies."

"I don't mean that."

Charlie drifted to the bench and dropped down beside Leo. "What do you mean, then?"

"Dunno." Leo took a swig from the rum bottle and offered it to Charlie, rolling his eyes when Charlie waved it away. "This town, I s'pose. You're all so fucking normal."

"Normal?"

"Yeah. Life happens here. Nothing good, nothing bad. It's boring."

Charlie laughed. "What did you expect? Tsunamis and nuclear war?"

"Piss off. Nah, I reckon I just thought it would be . . . something, you know?"

Charlie didn't know, but he said nothing, hoping that perhaps, for once, Leo would elaborate. And it seemed the rum had granted him his wish. Leo stretched his legs and let out the kind of whooshing sigh that told Charlie he had the weight of the world on his shoulders. "Swindon was shit, but I knew it like the back of my hand. This place is like another planet."

"A boring planet?"

Leo snorted. "Yep. Everywhere's boring, 'cept my head."

The words were muttered, and slightly slurred, but Charlie heard them like Leo had yelled them in his ear. He slid closer, hoping Leo would look at him, so he'd know for sure that he had no hope of ever knowing what Leo was thinking.

But Leo didn't look at him, so Charlie braved a tentative hand on his back. "There's still time for you to like this town. You haven't been here very long."

"Doesn't feel that way. Doesn't feel like anything."

"What do you mean?"

"Fucked if I know." Leo sighed and leaned back on the bench, but he didn't shrug away from Charlie's hand. "I don't know much anymore."

An eerie silence crept over them, enveloping them. For a long moment, Charlie welcomed it, like it could seep into Leo and absorb the pain he was trying so hard to mask with apathy. But it didn't work. Leo trembled, then exhaled with a stuttered gasp, and Charlie pulled Leo into his arms.

Leo fell sideways against him. Charlie wished Leo would cry, but Leo didn't cry. He lay slack in Charlie's loose embrace and stared up at the stars. "How did you know they really wanted you?"

"Hmm?" Charlie shifted. His chin touched Leo's hair. It tickled, and smelled of Leo—of smoke and rum—and the soft drizzle that had begun to moisten the heavy air around them. "You mean Mum and—uh—Kate and Reg?"

"Yeah."

"Because they didn't have to want me. They could've left me for someone else, or given me back any time things got rough, like the first couple who tried to adopt me."

Leo turned his head and fixed Charlie with a stare that suddenly didn't feel empty. A loaded gaze that pierced Charlie's soul and shook his bones. Warmth filled Charlie's veins, and an invisible chord drew him closer. Leo moved too, and then their lips touched . . . brushed against each other, gently at first, but then harder, like it meant something Charlie didn't quite understand, until, wide-eyed, Leo pulled away.

"What— What the fuck was that?"

"Nothing. I didn't do anything." Charlie wrenched himself free and stumbled off the bench. "I didn't do anything."

"Charlie—"

"No! Don't say it. I'm sorry. I'm sorry." Charlie backed away, then turned and fled, running across the park, his stomach in his mouth, churning and roiling, as humiliation and shame smothered him until he couldn't take another step.

Oh God.

What have I done?

Charlie sank to his knees on the wet grass. Silence once again enveloped him, but it was different this time. Without the sullen warmth of Leo beside him, it suffocated him like a fog of broken dreams.

He'd kissed Leo.

He'd *kissed* Leo, his vulnerable and messed-up foster brother who'd never given him any indication that he even liked boys that way, let alone liked *Charlie* that way.

The hate the year-eleven boys had thrown at him the day Leo had arrived echoed in his brain: *"Backs to the wall. Faggy Charlie might jump ya."*

Had they seen it all along? That it had only been a matter of time before he threw himself at someone who didn't want him?

Why, why, why?

What the fuck did I do? Dad had warned him that Leo's behaviour could get him sent away, but *this?*

God no. I can't be the reason he—

A harsh chuckle cut Charlie's thoughts dead. He blinked and squinted in the direction it had come from. Four familiar smirking faces greeted him. *Shit.* In his hurry to escape, he hadn't noticed the very same group of year elevens lurking by the skate ramps, a gang of no-good lads that even Wayne Murphy had the sense to avoid.

Darren Stroud got up. "Watcha doing over here?"

"Nothing." Charlie got up too and shoved his hands in his pockets. Was he going to get decked now? Did he care?

Not really.

"Why don't you come and do nothing with us, then? It's fun, boys, innit?"

Charlie shook his head. The lads at Darren's back sniggered, and Darren's grin widened to reveal a set of crooked, brown teeth that would be rotten by the time he hit twenty. "What about this, eh? Want some of this, emo boy?"

Darren opened his hand. Two pills sat, ghostlike, in his palm. Charlie stared at them. "I'm not an emo."

"Yeah? Prove it, faggy-boy."

Prove it? Piss off. Charlie resisted the urge to roll his eyes, but the harder he stared at the pills, the more the urge faded, and instead, a different energy swept over him. A compulsion that fought the lingering, burning sensation of Leo's lips on his. A compulsion that fought every instinct Charlie had ever known.

The compulsion won.

Charlie swiped the pills and swallowed them dry. They stuck in his throat, jagged and bitter, but he forced them down. Then he found Darren's gaze and shrugged. "Thanks for the drugs, dickhead."

NINE

What did I do? What did I do?

Leo sank back down on the bench as Charlie disappeared into the misty night. His heart screamed at him to follow, to pull Charlie back to him and kiss him again. To tell him, perhaps without words, that everything was going to be okay. But his heavy legs, hindered by too much rum and the cloud of hopelessness that was beginning to feel like his constant companion, wouldn't obey.

He brought a shaking hand to his mouth and traced his tingling lips with his fingertip. They felt raw and burned with the best kind of heat, but something was off.

Charlie's never done that before.

Leo tugged on his hair, knowing with a stomach-churning certainty that he was right. He'd recognised the fear in Charlie's eyes, because he'd seen it in his own, reflecting back at him the first time he'd snogged Lee McKensie after football training last year. The first time he'd truly realised that he didn't look at his friends the same way they looked at him.

Cold winter drizzle seeped into Leo's skin. He wrapped his arms around himself and shivered. The terror he'd felt that day had stayed with him a long time before real nightmares had taken its place. *I don't want Charlie to feel like that. I lo—*

"Leo!"

Leo jerked upright. His head spun. In his haze, he hadn't noticed it dropping to his knees. Someone shouted his name again, and then Wayne appeared out of the darkness, puffing laboured breaths of steam into the frosty air.

"Leo, mate. You gotta come with me. Your brother's dropped a bunch of mandy biscuits."

"*What?*" Leo jumped up and sprinted across the park, leaving Wayne far behind. *Mandy biscuits.* Leo knew the term all too well, but as the trees flew past, he held on to the faint hope that the posh kids in Heyton called their ecstasy pills something else.

But that hope was obliterated the moment he rounded the front of the cricket pavilion. He saw Lucy first, then Jess, both of them on their knees, bent over Charlie who was curled in a ball on the cold ground.

Leo bounded up the steps and pushed them aside. "What the fuck happened?"

"We don't know." Jess elbowed her way back to Charlie and pulled on his hood, trying to uncover his face. "We found him like this. Wayne said he took some pills from Darren Stroud."

"Who?" Leo looked around, but there was no one close by except Wayne, who was hovering at the edge of the grass.

"Darren Stroud," Jess repeated. "One of the year-eleven scumbags. Do you think he spiked Charlie's drink? Charlie doesn't do drugs. He never has."

"But he wasn't drinking either," Lucy said. "He said he didn't have any money."

Leo's stomach churned. He'd been the one with cash, and he'd spent it on rum he'd known Charlie wouldn't drink. Was this his fault? Had Charlie boshed a load of beans because Leo had been too selfish to share a few beers with him?

Lucy dropped her head. "What's that, Charlie, babe? Did you say something?"

Charlie abruptly uncurled himself. He straightened his legs and caught Leo's shin with a bruising kick as he scrambled to his feet. "Stop crawling on me."

"No one's crawling on you." Leo stood and held out his hands. "What did you take?"

Charlie stared at Leo's hands, head tilted to one side, eyes so wide the whites gleamed in the moonlight. Leo thought he hadn't heard him, but then Charlie laughed a laugh Leo had never heard from him before. "I love you."

For a brief moment, Leo's heart felt like it would burst out of his chest, then he realised that Charlie wasn't looking at him, he was gazing at Jess.

Jess stepped around Leo and took Charlie's hands. "You bloody idiot. What the hell have you taken?"

"Um . . ." Charlie stared up at the sky and blinked a few times. "Dunno. Do I look mashed?"

"And then some. We need to straighten you out before you go home. Your folks are going to hit the roof if they see you like this."

Charlie giggled. "Gimme a cuddle."

Jess obliged, and Leo relaxed a little. His own experiences with X had been less than pleasant, but he'd had some good times too. Good times he could barely remember now.

"Fucking hell, Charlie. Your heart's going mental."

Jess's startled exclamation made Leo jump. He stepped closer and took Charlie's wrist. Sure enough, his pulse was racing. "We should go home."

"Really?" Jess shifted uneasily. "Reg will go nuts. He'll probably call the old bill or something."

"It's okay." Leo pulled out his phone, retrieved one of only five contacts stored on it, and tapped out an SOS. "I know what to do."

———

It took some negotiating, but eventually, Leo managed to persuade the girls to let him take Charlie home. Charlie drifted beside him as Leo steered him through town. He seemed happy enough—more than happy—but Leo knew the effects of X well enough to know things could go wrong at any moment. What if the pills Charlie had taken weren't X at all? What if they'd been cut with weed killer or some shit? Leo's veins boiled with rage for the fuck-face who'd given Charlie the drugs, but his anger felt like nothing compared to the real fear that Charlie was about to drop dead.

"I love having you as my brother." Charlie stopped walking and turned to Leo with a soft, loopy grin. "You probably hate me because I tried to snog you, but I do love you."

Leo swallowed the lump that suddenly formed in his throat. "I don't hate you. Why would you think that?"

"'Cause you hate everyone, don't you? And, ya know, I did try and snog you and . . ."

"And?"

Charlie shrugged. "Dunno. I wanted to kiss you, though. I do that, with boys . . . I want to kiss them, instead of girls."

Leo's own heart quickened. "You like boys?"

"Yes." Charlie stared at Leo for a long moment, like he was waiting for Leo to say something—*anything*—but his attention was abruptly diverted before Leo found the words to tell him he wasn't alone in the world. "Ooh, Leo, look. The Christmas lights are still on the market cross. Let's go see."

He darted away before Leo could stop him. Leo caught up

to him by the stone steps that led to the focal point of Heyton's old high street. "Nah, no way. You're not climbing up there in this state. You'll break your bloody neck."

"But I want to see the lights," Charlie protested. He tried to free himself from Leo's restraining grip, but Leo held firm.

"There's no lights up there. You're tripping."

"Tripping? *Oh*, I get it. I like tripping."

Charlie stopped struggling and leaned against Leo. He was warm, like the open fire in the living room back in Swindon. "Come on," Leo said. "We need to go home."

Neither of them moved. Charlie's heartbeat thudded wildly against Leo's chest, and Leo's own pulse sped up, like it was chasing Charlie's. He sucked in a breath. His mouth was dry, and the memory of Charlie's lips on his hit him like a truck. "It's okay, Charlie."

"What is?" Charlie turned his head and stared at Leo, his usually keen gaze clouded by whatever chemicals were wreaking havoc in his blood. "You look all serious. I hate it when you look like that."

"Why?"

Charlie shrugged. "'Cause I know you hate it too."

"Fair enough." Leo forced himself to step away. "Come on. I mean it this time. We need to get home."

The rest of the walk was thankfully uneventful. Charlie's fascination with his surroundings faded, and by the time Fliss met them at the back door, he seemed more bewildered than anything else.

"For fuck's sake," Fliss said. "What the hell did he take?"

"Dunno. I wasn't there."

Fliss shot Leo a disbelieving glance as she guided Charlie into the house. "Yeah? So you didn't give him the pills?"

"Why would I do that and then text you for help? Sneak him in myself then, wouldn't I?"

"I don't know why you texted me at all. I'm not exactly a drugs guru."

Leo said nothing. He'd reached out to Fliss because he was scared shitless, and his gut had told him that she could help. There was no rhyme or reason, and he didn't much care if anyone thought he was a dirty drugs pusher . . . right?

Bullshit. If Reg gets wind of this, he'll kick you out for sure.

Panic surged in Leo's chest. Fliss shook him. "*Leo.*"

"What, *what?*"

Fliss glared, like she'd growled his name more than once. "Go and get some bananas from the dining room, and be *quiet.* Mum and Dad are watching TV in their room."

"Bananas?"

"Trust me." Fliss eyed Charlie, who was staring at the photos on the fridge door, singing to himself, and swaying like he didn't have a care in the world. "If we want him to sleep anytime before next Tuesday, he needs vitamins. Besides, have you got any better ideas?"

Leo fetched the bananas from the fruit bowl in the next room. When he got back, he was surprised to find Fliss and Charlie standing together by the kitchen window, arms around each other, like they really were siblings, instead of two people who simply lived in the same house.

"You're an idiot," Fliss said. "How many times have I told you not to take drugs?"

Charlie's grin was loopy. "I like drugs. They're fun."

"Won't be fun in the morning when your insides feel like sandpaper. Here, eat this, and drink some water. If your teeth stop chattering, I'll let you go to bed when you're done." Fliss handed Charlie one of Leo's retrieved bananas and filled a pint glass with water. Then, while Charlie did as he was told, she beckoned Leo to the kitchen doorway. "I think he's fine. If he was going to freak out or OD, he'd have done it by now. You'll need to keep him quiet, though, at least until the morning. Mum and Dad are taking Lila to Aunt Sal's first thing. They'll probably leave you two to sleep in, but keep an ear out, just in case. They can spot this shit a mile off."

Leo wondered how Fliss knew so much about drugs. He'd seen her stagger home from a night out with her mates more than once, but nothing to suggest that she caned anything harder than vodka. "You're sure he's okay?"

"As sure as I can be. I, uh . . ."

"What?"

Fliss shrugged. "I don't get it. Charlie's a good boy, you know? And he doesn't give a shit about impressing anyone. He didn't do this to look cool in front of his mates, so I reckon something happened to piss him off. Any ideas?"

Leo felt sick, but before he could answer, Charlie appeared beside him, eyes bright and slightly more focussed than they'd been since Leo had found him curled up on the ground. "Don't nag Leo, Fliss. He hates me already 'cause I kissed him."

Heat flooded Leo's cheeks, and the nausea tickling his belly got hotter and hotter until he felt like he would surely puke all over the weathered wood floor. But Fliss only shook her head and closed her eyes briefly. "I don't want to know what you two get up to in your spare time. Just don't get caught, okay? I can't be arsed with the drama. Now go to bed, the pair of you, and don't wake me up unless one of you is dying."

Fliss left them to it. Leo watched her go with an odd combination of relief and panic. Charlie called her a crazy bitch every other day, but Leo saw how strong she was, fearless and brave. Saw it in her eyes, in the steely glare that too often hid her kindest smile.

"Leeeooo." Charlie tapped Leo on the shoulder. "You're staring again. Come on. Fliss said we had to go to bed."

"Since when do you do what she tells you?" Leo shrugged

away and headed for the stairs, then thought better of it and tugged Charlie in front of him. "Hold on to the banister."

"It's pink."

Leo sighed. "If you say so. Just get upstairs. And do it quietly. I'm not hiding you from Reg."

The mention of Reg seemed to sober Charlie. He made his way upstairs and slipped into his bedroom without another sound. Leo followed him and shut the door behind them. The room was dark and cold. He flicked the light on, and Charlie turned towards him and smiled, and suddenly, the room felt like a summer's day.

Damn, that bloody smile.

Leo sat on the floor. Charlie appeared to be coming down from whatever crap he'd swallowed, but Leo was under no illusions that either of them would be sleeping anytime soon. He watched with heavy eyes as Charlie rummaged around under his bed, digging out piles of sketchbooks and pens. "What are you doing?"

"Looking for something."

"I figured that. What are you looking for?"

Charlie didn't answer, apparently distracted by a battered shoe box Leo had never seen before. He untied the string around it and took the lid off with more care than his jittery limbs should've allowed.

"Who's in the pictures?" Leo leaned forward, curious, in spite of the very real urge to curl up and sleep for a week.

Charlie held up a yellowed Polaroid. "Dunno. It could be my mum, or an aunt, maybe. What do you think?"

Leo squinted at the photograph. The young woman had long dark hair and deep brown eyes—*Charlie's* eyes. Mother or not, they shared blood. "You look like her. Where did you get these from?"

"The orphanage closed down a few years ago. One of the

missionary workers sent a box of stuff to Kate. Not sure any of it's really mine, though. Could be anyone's."

"She doesn't look like just anyone."

"Whatever." Charlie shrugged in a way that made Leo feel like he was staring at his own reflection, until Charlie's pensive frown cleared as though it had never been there at all. He rummaged in the box again, and then grinned manically as he retrieved two colourful beaded bracelets. "Oh, hey. I'd forgotten about these."

Leo snagged a bracelet and turned it over in his hands. "Nice."

"Yeah?" Charlie jammed the lid on the shoe box and shoved it under his bed. "Have it, then. Make up for me chewing your face off earlier."

Charlie left the room before Leo found a coherent response. He clattered around in the bathroom before returning in a pair of pyjama bottoms that looked suspiciously like he'd fished them out of the washing basket, no T-shirt, and the remaining bracelet around his left wrist. He didn't glance Leo's way as he drifted to his bed and sat down. Leo wondered what he was thinking. Wished he'd tell him, and then felt horrified that he might.

What are you so scared of?

Leo honestly didn't know. "Do you think you can sleep?"

"Hmm?" Charlie tore his gaze from the wall. "Um, maybe, if the wall stops dancing. What about you? You've still got your jeans on."

"So?"

"Why do you wear so many clothes in bed?"

In case I have to get up and run. "'Because it's winter and this house is fucking freezing."

"No, it's not. Mum leaves the heating on twenty-four hours a day 'cause she hates the thought of any of us feeling cold."

"Whatever." Yearning for his own bed, Leo cast a longing glance at the open door, then crawled across the room and took Charlie's wrist. "You don't seem as trashed now."

Charlie sniggered. "Must be the magic bananas."

"Magic something." Leo released Charlie's wrist, satisfied his pulse had slowed enough for Leo to leave him—

"Are you going to move out?"

Leo jumped. He hadn't noticed Charlie casually invading his personal space. "What?"

"You know, to escape the gay boy."

"Gay boy?" Leo laughed, couldn't help it. "What good would that do?"

Charlie flinched. "You don't have to be a dick about it. I said I was sorry."

"I don't want you to be sorry." Leo turned away.

Charlie caught his face in his heated palm. "Why?"

"Because—" Leo stopped, the words he'd never uttered aloud stuck in his throat. "Because I liked it, all right? I liked you kissing me, because I like what you like . . . I like *you*, and I like boys, but I don't want to talk about it. I want you to be okay, and I want to sleep, and I can't—"

Charlie silenced Leo with a kiss that was very different from that first tentative brush of lips in the park. Those kisses had felt like ghosts. A whisper of something neither of them quite understood. And Charlie hadn't touched him then, hadn't pulled him close, or grazed his cheek with his electric fingertips.

But he did those things now, and enveloped Leo in a tight embrace, holding him so fiercely that Leo had never felt safer, even before Dennis had drunk the devil into all of them.

For a long, dizzying moment, Leo stood stock-still, frozen in the fire of Charlie's kiss, then he snapped, broke free, and pushed Charlie onto his bed, kissing him back so hard their teeth clashed.

Charlie grunted and pulled back, though he kept his arms around Leo. "Oops."

"Yeah." Leo sucked in a harsh breath. *Damn.* How had they gone from a tipsy night out at the park, to snogging on Charlie's bed? Did it even matter? With Charlie wrapped around him, warming him, inside and out, Leo couldn't find the will to care.

"You're shivering." Charlie suddenly scooted back. "Get under the duvet."

In the blink of a bleary eye, Leo found himself in Charlie's bed, curled up on his side, his legs tangled with Charlie's and his head on his chest. He opened his mouth, shut it again, and then yawned so hard his jaw cracked. "I'm so fucking tired."

"I know, Leo. Go to sleep. I'll protect you. I promise."

TEN

Charlie woke to a groan that sounded like it came from a dying animal. He blinked and peeled his tongue from the roof of his mouth. *Shit, was that me?* A glance at Leo sleeping beside him confirmed that it must have—

Whoa.

He looked down again and registered the warmth of Leo's body seeping into his own.

What the fuck?

The events of the night before slammed into his brain—the kiss, the pills, neon lights, and more kissing—

Oh my God.

Charlie flushed. He'd kissed Leo. He'd taken drugs—dirty bloody street drugs. And he'd *kissed Leo.* Multiple times, at intervals he couldn't quite remember.

Oh. My. God.

Charlie licked his lips. They were cracked and sore, like he'd chewed on them all night, and mortification washed over him. How trashed must he have been for Leo get into bed with him? His brain was scrambled and out of order—sketchy memories fused with recollections that couldn't be real—but he remembered Leo's gaze following his every move, staring at him like he was a ticking bomb. Remembered Leo's guiding hands, warm on his back, his arm, his wrists.

And Charlie remembered the heat in Leo's eyes when he'd admitted that he liked kissing Charlie.

Footsteps on the stairs startled Charlie out of his hazy reverie. The light tread sounded like Kate.

Shit.

Charlie scrambled out of bed and darted across the landing. He dove under Leo's duvet just as Kate reached the doorway.

Kate blinked and glanced out into the hallway, clearly checking Charlie's room. "What are you doing in here?"

"We swapped for a joke."

"What joke?"

"Um . . ."

"Never mind." Kate looked over her shoulder again. "What time did you go to sleep? Lila wants to say good-bye before we go to Aunt Sal's, but I don't want to wake Leo if you had a late night."

"It wasn't too late. Half ten, maybe?" Charlie said, though in truth he had no idea what time he'd gone to sleep. In fact, he couldn't remember sleeping at all. Only lying in bed with Leo, holding him close, and wishing he could chase the darkness from his eyes.

"Charlie?"

"Hmm?"

Kate frowned. "Are you all right? You're a bit pale."

"I'm fine."

"Well, you don't seem it. Listen, your father and I like to trust you to put yourselves to bed at a reasonable hour at the weekends, but we're not idiots. If you're going to start staying up all night playing Xbox or whatever it is you boys do, we'll have to impose a bedtime."

Charlie thought about scoffing, but Kate's glare kept him quiet, along with Reg's dire warning about what would happen if Leo's behaviour became too disruptive. *Quick. Think of something she likes.* "Leo played football in the park. He's probably tired from that."

Kate's expression brightened. "Oh that's nice. We were hoping he'd start playing again now his arm is a little better. Anyway, we're off to Aunt Sal's for the day. I've left cold pizzas and salad downstairs for lunch. Try and amuse yourselves without making a mess, okay? We'll be back around six."

Kate left. Charlie pushed aside the guilt that came with his white lie and waited for the front door to slam, and then the car to roll off the drive before he hauled himself out of Leo's bed and went back to his room. He retrieved his phone from the tangled pile of clothes on the floor. Twenty messages from Jess and Lucy greeted him. He fired off a couple of replies, reassuring them he wasn't dead, then shuffled to the bathroom to make a half-hearted attempt to clean himself up.

Taking a shower felt like a mountain he couldn't climb, so he settled for taking a leak and brushing his teeth, and then scrutinising the cracked skin on his lips and the dark circles under his eyes. Damn, he was a bloody mess after just one mad night. No wonder junkies looked so utterly ruined.

He drifted back to his bedroom with heavy legs. Leo hadn't moved an inch. Charlie considered him, and then the empty bed across the landing. He shivered, remembering the warmth of Leo pressed against him, and before he knew it, found himself sliding back into his own bed.

Couldn't quite find the nerve to snuggle into Leo again, though. Instead, he snagged his headphones from his bedside table and found a crap film on Netflix to doze to while he waited for Leo to wake up.

He was on his second film by the time Leo finally rolled

over and tucked his bad arm close to his chest, grimacing as he opened his eyes.

Charlie pulled his headphones out. "All right?"

Leo rubbed his face. "Shouldn't I be asking you that?"

"Dunno." Charlie took in Leo's heavy lidded eyes and flushed cheeks. He put a hand on Leo's forehead. "You look pretty rough, and you're burning up."

"Am I?" Leo grunted.

Charlie frowned. "Actually, yes, you are. Do you feel okay?"

Leo shook his head. Charlie waited for him to elaborate, but Leo didn't do anything other than stare into space, his expression vacant in a way Charlie hadn't seen before.

Charlie touched his shoulder and felt the heat simmering beneath his skin. "What's the matter?"

"I . . . um, I feel like shit."

All at once, Leo seemed incredibly young. He'd had bad days before—days when his arm had bothered him, or his mood had grown so black he'd refused to leave his bed—but this felt different. Charlie set his phone aside and slid down the bed so his face was level with Leo and asked again, softer this time, almost in a whisper, "What's the matter? Are you gonna puke?"

"No, nothing like that. Just a headache, and my throat hurts."

"That's probably the twenty fags you smoked last night, and the bottle of rum." Charlie chanced a grin.

Leo stared back at him. "Why did you do it?"

"Do what?" Charlie tore his gaze from Leo's and focused on a tiny speck of fluff on the pillow beyond Leo's head. "Kiss you, or drop the pills?"

"The pills, Charlie. I know why you kissed me. We talked about it last night."

A flashback of Leo's flat confession flickered into Charlie's mind—*he liked me kissing him*—but he pushed it away. Leo was right, they'd talked about that already, and stretched out together in bed, nose to nose, feet touching, Charlie wasn't sure he had the balls to talk about it again.

That left the pills, but it was far from the easy option. What was he supposed to say? *I kissed you, you backed away, and I wanted to forget it forever. . .* It sounded pathetic, even in his head. "You do drugs all the time. What do you care?"

"I smoke a bit of weed. I don't do nothin' else."

"But you have, though, right?" Charlie flicked his gaze back to Leo. "You've done them all, haven't you?"

"Nope, but if I had, don't you think I'd still be doing them if they were any good? Drugs are bullshit. You don't need them. You're not crazy like me."

"Crazy?"

"Yeah, I've got pills for that, you know." Leo rolled his eyes briefly into the back of his head before he closed them. "To help me sleep, or some shit. They don't work though. Reckon I'd need to drop ten of them to silence the dead."

"The dead?"

"Yeah, 'cept the dead are never really silent, are they? Not in your dreams."

Charlie swallowed the lump in his throat. Some nights it seemed like he lived every moment of Leo's nightmares, but he knew there were many that Leo suffered in silence, or evaded by staying awake all night long, sitting on the roof, or the window sill, blowing clouds of smoke to the stars. "I'm sorry."

"Hmm?" Leo opened his eyes. "What are *you* sorry for?"

"I'm sorry you're so unhappy."

Charlie started to roll away, but Leo caught his face in his heated palm. "I'm not unhappy."

"Yes, you are."

"I'm not. Not here . . . not with you."

Charlie took a breath, but whatever response he might have

made was cut off by Leo's lips on his, tentative at first, but then harder—*much* harder than they'd kissed in the park.

And harder than Charlie had dreamed of in the moments he'd drifted off while waiting for Leo to wake.

The kiss went on and on, grew deeper with every brush of lips and stuttered gasp. Charlie's blood roared in his ears and his skin tingled. His heart quickened until he was sure he'd combust. He thought he'd kissed Leo before, thought he remembered how it felt, but his disjointed recollection had nothing on reality. Kissing Leo was like flying, and Charlie didn't want to come down—

Leo pulled away with a soft groan. "Oh God, my head."

The fog cleared from Charlie's brain. He blinked and took in Leo's renewed pallor. "Shit, okay. Lie down. I'll get you some paracetamol from Mum's room."

"Don't go." Leo tightened his grip on Charlie's wrists. "I'm fine, honest."

"Humour me." Charlie tugged on the pillow and gave Leo a gentle push. "I'll be right back."

He got up and hurried to Kate and Reg's room. Kate kept all medications locked away, but she always left a single dose of over-the-counter painkillers where older kids could find them.

Charlie took them back to Leo with a glass of water. "Swallow."

Leo raised an eyebrow. "Wanna rephrase that?"

"Hmm? Oh, um . . ." Heat flooded Charlie's cheeks.

Leo chuckled, though it sounded bone-tired. "Never mind." He swallowed the pills, then laid his hand on Charlie's bare chest almost absently, before he blinked and let it drop. "This should feel weird."

"Huh?"

"This." Leo gestured between them. "You were so fucked

up last night, I thought you'd be a basket case this morning, but this . . . it feels like we always do it."

Charlie's heart did a strange flip, like Leo's hand had turned it upside down and shaken it. "We're not really doing anything. You've been asleep all morning."

"You know what I mean."

Charlie thought he did, but Leo was making him nervous, making him doubt every assumption that ran through his mind. Was Leo saying he wanted to kiss him again? Or that kissing him was so boring it felt mundane? Charlie took a chance and reached for Leo's hand, brushing his thumb over Leo's thrumming pulse. Leo grinned a little, leaning forward, and—

The door opened. Fliss looked in with a smirk that made Charlie want to punch her in the face. "Morning, boys. Not interrupting, am I?"

Charlie slithered off the bed as Leo dropped back on the pillows. "What do you want?"

"What do you think? I'm checking you didn't fry your brains last night."

"What? How do you even know about that?" Charlie glared at Leo. "Did you tell her?"

"Er—"

"Oh, please," Fliss cut in. "What was he supposed to do? Leave you to climb up on the roof and cuddle the stars? Someone had to straighten you out."

Cuddling the stars was probably the most poetic thing Charlie had ever heard Fliss say, but the idea of her "straightening" him out was all kinds of freaky, especially combined with the way she was glancing between him and Leo. *She knows.* "I'm fine."

"Good," Fliss snapped. "What the hell were you thinking? You're the good kid. It would break Mum's heart if you turned into a druggie."

"I'm not a bloody druggie, Fliss. It was a one-off. I'm not going to do it again, so you can save your lecture. Besides, it's not like you give a shit."

"*Charlie.*" Leo punched Charlie's leg. "Don't be a dick."

"Don't worry about it," Fliss said before Charlie could respond. "He's right. I don't give a shit. I just want some peace around here, and I won't get that with him pissing about with drugs. Have a good day, little ones. I'm going out."

She left, slamming the door behind her. Charlie cut his gaze to Leo. "She does my head in."

"So? Doesn't mean she doesn't care." Leo rolled onto his side with life in his eyes that Charlie hadn't seen since he'd woken up. "You're too hard on each other."

Charlie sat on the edge of the bed. "I didn't think you cared much either."

Leo grunted. "I don't care if you tear lumps off Fliss. It's just pointless *and* stupid. She didn't have to help you last night—she could've let you get caught—but she didn't. She fed you bananas and gave you a hug. Trust me, mate—she cares."

Bananas? Hugs? Is he for real? "Thought we weren't calling each other 'mate'?"

Leo smiled one of his too-rare smiles. "I changed my mind. You can call me whatever you like. Now, are we watching *X-Men* or not?"

All of a sudden, Charlie felt as exhausted as Leo looked, and it was almost too easy to crawl into bed with him, load the movie onto his laptop, and lie down. After a few minutes, Leo shuffled close and laid his head on Charlie's shoulder.

"I do care, you know . . . about you, and Lila. Can't help it. Just wish it didn't hurt so much."

Charlie turned slightly, wishing he could meet Leo's eyes without dislodging his head. "What hurts?"

"Life, Charlie. You'll see."

ELEVEN

Leo sank into the couch, pulling Charlie with him, their lips still fused together, dancing a dance that always started so slow and sweet—tentative—only to end like this: heavy and heady, with them tangled together, gasping for breath.

Charlie broke away with a soft smile, and Leo grinned right back, a gentle wave washing over him, sweeping away the monsters in his mind. Sweeping away everything but the tingling in his lips and limbs. Kissing Charlie was like that.

Addictive.

Thrilling.

Kissing Charlie was magic, and he couldn't get enough.

Their lips met again. Leo wrapped his arms around Charlie's lean back and held him close, debating whether he had the nerve to slide his hands under Charlie's Marvel T-shirt to feel his skin. He'd spent more time than he cared to admit wondering if it was as perfect as it looked, as flawless and smooth. It probably was. Everything else about Charlie seemed to be.

Leo took a chance and repositioned his hands on Charlie's waist, edging them under the hem of Charlie's T-shirt. Warm skin greeted him, laced over sinuous muscle and the hard, knotted bones of Charlie's spine. He moved his hands higher and higher, until he could feel Charlie's every breath and thudding heartbeat, and his head swam as Charlie deepened their kiss, swirling his tongue into Leo's mouth, and clutching Leo's shoulders tight enough to leave a bruise.

Bloody hell.

Why had they waited so long? All those silent weeks, broken only by monosyllabic grunts, or the occasional strained conversation. All those weeks wasted when they could've been doing *this*.

Charlie dug his nails into Leo's skin, interrupting his wandering mind. Leo sucked in a breath and arched into him, sure he'd explode. They were about to reach the precipice they'd visited many times over the last few days, that hazy, heated place where kissing morphed into a swirling vortex that wasn't quite enough.

Leo's heart quickened. He'd never truly contemplated what came next, had never dared, but Charlie did something to him— something that tumbled all the barriers of doubt and ignorance. Something that made him want *more*.

He pulled away, breaking their lips apart, and lost himself in Charlie's liquid gaze, those soulful eyes that seemed to go on forever. "Do you want—"

The front door slammed. Charlie's eyes widened, and he slid off the couch like he'd never been there at all. "Shit, that's Dad. Turn the telly on."

Leo blinked and forced himself upright, straightening his clothes, and hoping the heat in his cheeks was imagined. He fumbled for the remote, and the TV came to life, blasting the room with whatever R&B crap Fliss had been dancing around to before she'd left for work.

Charlie flung himself into an armchair just as Reg reached the doorway. "All right, Dad?"

"So, so," Reg said. "What are you two up to?"

"Watching telly," Charlie said.

Reg glanced at the TV and raised an eyebrow. "Sure about that? Doesn't seem like your kind of thing."

"Like you'd know," Leo said. "Charlie loves all that Usher shit."

"Language, Leo," Reg said, though he seemed amused by the glare Charlie tossed at Leo. "Anyway, regardless of what I do and don't know about your taste in music, I know what mischief looks like, so whatever you two have been up to, you'd better not have made a mess."

Charlie kept his gaze firmly on the TV, so Leo shrugged. "We haven't made a mess."

"Good," Reg said. "Right, Leo, I need to borrow you for a moment, then you can get back to whatever you weren't doing before I came home."

Leo begrudgingly hauled himself off the sofa and followed Reg into the kitchen. "What have I done?"

"Nothing that I know of," Reg said mildly. "I wanted to let you know your follow-up appointment with the burn specialist came through. It's in a few weeks."

"Oh." Leo's stomach turned over, reclaiming the nausea he'd only just shifted from his weird illness the week before.

Reg turned away and filled the kettle. "I can imagine that the prospect of another operation is frightening, Leo, but it might not come to that. The consultant said the old graft might correct itself."

"I heard what he said."

Reg said nothing, and for a moment, the only sound in the room was the hiss of the boiling kettle. Then he moved to the table and pulled out two chairs, gesturing for Leo to sit.

Leo sat, and Reg went on, "I don't want to harp on about what happened last time we went to the hospital, but you have to know it's nothing to be ashamed of. Plenty of people who haven't been through half of what you've endured have much worse reactions to serious injury."

"I didn't react. Just felt sick, that's all."

"Fair enough." Reg let out a soft sigh. "But talking of feeling sick, Kate reckons you've looked under the weather all week. Is there anything we can do for you?"

"Nah." Leo pushed back his chair with a harsh scrape. "I'm fine, so you can leave me alone."

Leo escaped the kitchen as fast as he could without running. For once, he'd told Reg the truth. He *did* feel fine, aside from the heat building in his injured arm, woken by flashbacks of his visit to Dr. Frankenstein. Whatever had laid him low last weekend was fading too, erased by the distraction of Charlie's magical kisses.

Shame Charlie had disappeared from the living room by the time Leo got back.

Tuesday afternoon was officially the dullest part of Leo's week. Double chemistry with Mr. Lanning, the most boring man in the world with a voice to match. Today, Leo let the droning wash over him and laid his head on his folded arms, closing his eyes, and on cue, Charlie popped into his head. His eyes, his inky hair. His shy, crooked smile and the lush smooth skin Leo had spent most of the previous evening exploring with his fingertips. He had Charlie's back committed to memory now. *I wonder if his chest—*

Wayne kicked him under the table, and murmured from behind his hand. "What are you grinning about?"

Was I grinning? Leo had no idea. He schooled his features into the insolent smirk Wayne likely expected from him. "I'm not grinning, I'm dying over here."

"Old Lanning ain't so bad. Rather his shitty lesson than that history crap we've got tomorrow."

Leo sighed. "This isn't a lesson, it's torture. If Lanning wasn't a teacher, he'd be a prison guard."

"Nah." Wayne sniggered. "Lanning's not that interesting."

"Quiet." Mr. Lanning knocked his fist on the table right by Leo's head. "I won't tell you two again."

Great. Leo rolled his eyes and let them fall closed. Damn. It wasn't enough to be bored; they had to be *quiet* and bored, silent. Like the dead . . ." "'*Cept the dead are never really silent, are they? Not in your dreams.*"

Leo sat up sharply, his pleasant musings forgotten. He remembered muttering those words the night Charlie had dropped the X pills, but for the life of him, he couldn't remember why. That seemed to happen when he was with Charlie. His brain and his tongue were far too in tune with each other, and yet conversely disconnected.

In other words, he said shit he didn't mean to say, *all* the fucking time.

Charlie, Charlie, Charlie.

Leo tried to pull his thoughts back to that liquid place where there was nothing but Charlie and the sweetly clean scent of his skin, but the flickering of a Bunsen burner in his peripheral vision caught his attention. He frowned, glancing about to see he'd somehow missed *every* Bunsen burner in the room being lit, even the one right in front of him.

The blue-orange glow sucked him in, muting the world around him to the faint, persistent hiss of the gas tap. He stopped breathing through his nose, but the smell filled his lungs and he tasted smoke on his tongue.

And then it burned his throat. Leo coughed as familiar heat spread through his ruined arm, tingling, smouldering on the scars, and then oozing out, creeping into every muscle and nerve, getting hotter and hotter, until he heard his skin crackle and smelled the stomach-churning stench of scorched flesh.

Leo swallowed and searched frantically for something—anything—to shield him from the brutal flashback that was coming. Him and Lila screaming, burning, running. Hurling open the kitchen door, only for strong hands to push them back.

"No, you don't, boy. You can rot with your ma—"

Wayne kicked Leo again. "'Ere, look out. There's the tool that spiked your brother."

Somehow, Leo followed Wayne's gaze through the classroom window. A lanky boy was drifting across the courtyard, hood up, hands in his pockets. Leo didn't recognise him, but rage spread through his veins, a wildfire of fury far hotter than the agonising burn in his arm. His eyes narrowed, and his warped perspective tilted. The image of Wendy, broken and bleeding on the kitchen floor, morphed, her hair darkening until it was no longer ash-blonde and blood-stained, and instead inky locks flopped over a face that wasn't hers.

Charlie.

Leo pushed his chair back. It tipped and clattered to the floor, but he paid it no heed, jumping over it and dashing to the classroom door. The buzz of surprise behind him barely registered, Mr. Lanning's exasperated bellow even less. Leo ran away from it all and charged down the corridor to the side doors that led outside. He threw them open, scanning the courtyard for the drippy figure in the hood and spotted him by the gate.

Got you.

Leo sprinted across the courtyard, fists raised, and collided with the boy at full pelt, landing a quick succession of blows to his face and ribs. The boy grunted in shock, then cried out, gasping, as Leo kicked him in the stomach, and sent him sprawling to the ground.

"Get up, dickhead." Leo grabbed the boy's blazer and yanked him upright. "I'm just getting started."

"Wha—" The boy raised his hands clearly in bewilderment rather than self-defence. "Who the fuck are you? What's your problem, mate?"

"I ain't your mate." Leo pulled his fist back and struck the boy again, splitting his lip. "And it don't matter who I am. I'm going to fuck you up."

The boy's eyes widened. Then he seemed to shake himself, and he scrambled to his feet. "Yeah? Come on, then."

Leo grinned and sprang forward. The boy tried to block Leo's blows, but instead of punching him, Leo grabbed his arms and forced them apart. He tipped his own head back, then flung it hard, putting all his weight and strength behind a head butt that sent the boy back to the ground.

The boy didn't get up this time. In fact, he didn't move at all. Leo pulled his foot back to kick him back to life, but two sets of arms clamped around him from behind, one at his waist, the other at his shoulders, restraining him in a hold so tight he could hardly breathe.

"Enough!" Mr. Griggs shouted as another teacher dropped to the ground to shield the other boy. "Break it up. Come on, lad. Inside with you. You're going straight to the head's office and likely home after that. You're in big trouble, Mr. Hendry. Mark my words. *Big* trouble."

TWELVE

Charlie shuffled out of his geography lesson arm in arm with Jess. "So you bunked off school with Callum and went to his house?"

"Not *his* house, Charlie," Jess said. "I told you. We went to his nan's bungalow."

"And what did you do there?" Charlie braced himself, knowing she'd tell him every detail whether he wanted them or not. "Please tell me his nan wasn't in?"

Jess huffed. "Course she wasn't. She does Meals on Wheels on Mondays. We had the place to ourselves. Good job, too. We spent all day in bed."

"You shagged him in his nan's bed? Jess, that's *nasty*."

"Who are you? The moral police?" Jess rolled her eyes. "Besides, I didn't shag him. Not yet, at least. He doesn't want to until after my birthday."

"Probably best." Charlie had heard that half the kids in the year above were already having sex, whether they'd turned sixteen or not, but the idea of being caught doing that sent the wrong kind of shiver down his spine.

"Charlie?"

"Hmm?" Charlie glanced at Jess to find her staring intently at him. "What?"

"Would you tell me if you had a girlfriend?"

"A girlfriend? Where the hell would I get one of those around here?"

"What about a boyfriend instead?"

Charlie stopped walking. "What?"

"Oh, come on, Charlie. Don't be embarrassed. I like boys. Why shouldn't you?"

"What makes you think I like boys?"

Jess shrugged. "I'm not saying that you do, just that it's—you know—okay if you—"

"Charlie!"

Dazed, Charlie whirled around, instantly pulled out of the conversation he was *definitely* not ready to have. Wayne Murphy was bearing down on him, his perpetually sweaty face flushed, his dull eyes uncharacteristically wild. *Damn. Is he finally going to deck me?* Charlie braced himself, ready to fight back as much as he could without lowering himself to Wayne's level.

But the impact of Wayne crashing into him never came. Wayne skidded to a stop in front of him and grabbed Charlie's arms. "You gotta get to reception. Leo's flipped his shit."

"He's what?"

"He's lost it, mate. Booted it out of science and kicked the shit out of Darren Stroud in the courtyard. Proper battered him."

Charlie's blood ran cold. Darren Stroud ruled year eleven and made Wayne look like a bloody prefect. *Oh God.* The chill in Charlie's veins turned to ice, and real fear lanced his heart. Leo hadn't said much about *that* night, but he'd made no attempt to hide the anger in his eyes whenever Charlie had pondered the source of the most idiotic thing he'd ever done. "Where is he? What happened?"

"I just told you," Wayne said. "He flipped. One minute he was pretty much asleep, next he was outside smashing up Stroud. Griggs dragged him off and to the office, but Leo looked like he was gonna batter him too, so I reckon you should get down there. He ain't so bad when he's with you."

Charlie didn't need telling twice, even if Wayne's observation was so astute that he had to wonder if he'd been dropped onto another planet.

He pushed past Wayne and left Jess behind, dashing through the corridors and out of the maths building. The main office was on the other side of the school, and as he ran, there were signs of a major incident all around him—teachers milling about with walkie-talkies, clusters of kids congregated in places that usually held little interest. Blood on the concrete in the courtyard—

Charlie stumbled. *Is that Leo's blood?* But that theory didn't fit with what Wayne had told him. If he was to be believed, then it was far more likely that the shiny red streaks belonged to Darren Stroud, and for some reason that was no comfort as Charlie pushed on.

Besides, Wayne Murphy was full of shit. There was every chance that he'd fed Charlie a load of rubbish.

But the moment Charlie burst into reception, it was clear that Wayne had told him the truth. Leo was nowhere in sight, but Darren Stroud was there—in bits on the visitor's couch. Broken. Bleeding. And being tended to by a paramedic. Horrified, Charlie's hands flew to his mouth. *Leo. What have you done?*

And *why* had he done it? Charlie couldn't deny there was a fire simmering in Leo that he was nowhere close to understanding, but this?

Charlie's heart hurt. This wasn't Leo. It couldn't be.

"Charlie?"

Charlie jumped. Mrs. Parkin grasped his shoulders and turned him gently to face her. "Are you okay, sweetheart?"

"Where's Leo?"

"I was about to ask you that."

"What do you mean?"

Mrs. Parkin frowned slightly. "Exactly what I said. Leo's in a lot of trouble, and he's only made it worse for himself by running off."

"Leo's not here? I thought he'd be in the office."

"He was, but he disappeared when Mr. Griggs left him to fetch another teacher."

"Where did he go?"

"We don't know, Charlie. That's why I was on my way to find you. Leo doesn't know the school very well yet. Is there anywhere you think he'd go when he's upset?"

It was a rare day that Leo wasn't upset, and Charlie couldn't recall him ever finding sanctuary at school. And even if he could think of a place where Leo might have been, would he rat him out? Could he?

Charlie's stomach did an uncomfortable flip, and his fingers automatically drifted to the bracelet on his wrist—the one that matched the brightly coloured beads Leo often wore over the bandage on his injured arm. Unbidden, his mind treated him to the image of Leo's ruined flesh and new panic set in. "Is Leo okay? Is he hurt?"

Mrs. Parkin shook her head. "We don't know. He wouldn't let Mr. Griggs check."

Of course he wouldn't. Leo hated men—all men, even Reg. Especially Reg. There was no way he'd let a burly brute like Mr. Griggs put his hands on him. "What are you going to do? Have you called my mum?"

"There's no answer at home, so we've sent a message to her phone, asking her to call the school. Do you know if she's around today? We're about to call your father."

Charlie thought of Reg taking that call and shuddered. Reg hated violence. He wouldn't let Andy watch the boxing at home. *Oh God. What if he sends Leo away?*

Nausea finally overwhelmed Charlie, and he sank into a nearby chair. Kate and Reg gave each kid they took every chance in the world, but only if the rest of the family was safe from harm. Would they see Leo's attack on Darren as a threat to them all?

I have to find him.

Nausea forgotten, Charlie lurched to his feet. Mrs. Parkin stepped back, eyeing him in the same way that teachers usually eyed Leo. "Where are you going, Charlie?"

"Toilet," he said, looking past her for an avenue of escape. "I need to text my brother too. He might've heard from Leo. They're—um—close."

Charlie had never been much of a liar, and the sense that Mrs. Parkin saw right through him made it hard not to squirm under the weight of her suspicious frown.

But his squeaky-clean record perhaps worked in his favour. She stepped back and waved him away. "Okay, Charlie. Go to the bathroom, then contact your brother and see if he knows anything. It's very important that we find Leo, and I don't want to bother your father at work."

Charlie would've agreed to just about anything to escape. He appeased Mrs. Parkin as much as he could, and then made his escape, fleeing the office and dashing across the courtyard to the nearest block with toilets. Once inside, where Mrs. Parkin couldn't see him, he cut through a classroom, retrieved his bike, and slipped out of a side gate. Leo wasn't at school. Charlie didn't know how he knew, but he did. Leo was long gone, and Charlie felt every ripple of his distress like a knife to the heart.

I have to find him.

But where to start? Leo wouldn't have gone home, which left the park, and the sacred place under the bridge where Charlie had taken him the first time he'd been upset at school. This was nothing like that, but the canal called Charlie's name. *That's it. He has to be there.*

Charlie rode like the wind to the black bridge and ditched his bike on the path. He scrambled down beneath the bridge, where the water was murkiest, half expecting to find Leo exactly where he'd sat all those weeks ago, but the small clearing was empty. Devoid of anything, save a grubby, blood-smeared bandage.

THIRTEEN

I'm just like him. I'm just like him. I'm just like him.

Leo pressed his fists into his eye sockets and rocked back and forth, reliving the other boy's bones crunching against his knuckles over and over as he rained blows down on him—punching and kicking. Revelling in his pain. Enjoying it. Embracing the sick satisfaction as it spread through his veins.

I'm just like him—

Fuck.

I am him.

The realisation burned through him like wildfire, roaring up his throat from his stomach. He ripped his hands from his face and lurched sideways, vomiting onto the dusty ground. The other boy's blood swam before his eyes, and it was all he could do to stay upright. To not crumple and be at one with the dirt where he belonged.

I want Charlie.

But he couldn't have Charlie, because he didn't deserve him. Charlie was good, kind, and pure. And Leo was evil . . . like Dennis.

I'll hurt him. I'll hurt Lila.

I have to go.

Leo scrambled to his feet. His coat dragged on the ground, hanging off his good arm. He shrugged it off and hurled it in the vague direction of a nearby bin, but paid no heed to where it landed, distracted by his damaged arm. Exposed to the bitterly cold air, it was weeping blood and the strange clear fluid that frightened him so much. In the past, he'd imagined that it was his soul crying for Wendy. Now he knew that it was what remained of him seeping away, leaving nothing in its wake but every damned gene Dennis had given him.

I hate him.

I am him.

I have to go.

Leo closed his eyes, searching for any strand of peace amongst the chaos in his brain. But he found nothing except absolute certainty that Heyton was the wrong place for him to be. Lila, Charlie, they were better off without him.

Resolved, he opened his eyes and ditched the park. Leaving Lila without saying good-bye broke what was left of his burned-out heart, but there was no other way. Even dazed as he was, he knew that going back to the house was a bad move. He'd heard the sirens, and he'd never forget the mess he'd left behind at school. *No.* He couldn't go back. Not now. Not ever.

There was only one home left for him.

***

Charlie paced the hallway, straining his ears to eavesdrop on the crisis meeting going on in the living room. Reg, Kate, social workers . . . the police, they were all there, and had been since Charlie had finally admitted defeat and gone home with Leo's grubby bandage stuffed in his pocket.

He'd yet to admit that he'd found it by the canal, but then, once it had become clear that he'd returned home alone, no one had asked him anything else, and that was making him nervous. Did Kate and Reg know that Charlie and Leo spent every spare moment huddled up in bed, kissing the hell out of each other? Were they waiting for the police and social workers to leave before they forced Charlie to confess?

Nah. If they do know, they won't care until Leo's home.

If Leo was *allowed* home. Charlie had seen foster siblings disappear from his life over crimes less severe than the beating Leo had inflicted on Darren Stroud—broken nose, cracked ribs, a possible concussion. *"He could've killed him,"* one of the social workers had said. No one had argued.

The front door opened. Heart in his mouth, Charlie spun on his heel, but it wasn't Leo—it was Fliss, her expression as grim as Charlie had ever seen it.

She rounded on him before she'd undone her coat. "If you know where he is, you have to tell them. This serious, Charlie."

"I don't know where he is."

"Real talk? Are you sure about that? Because I haven't told Mum and Dad that you and Leo are together, but I will if I think you're doing anything to make this horrible shit worse."

Charlie blinked. "We're not together."

"Whatever. I don't care. Just don't play any silly games. You'll only make it worse for him."

"What do you mean?"

Fliss inclined her head towards the living room. "What do you think they're talking about in there? Do you think they're having a nice little meeting about increasing Leo's art therapy and taking him to church more?"

"No one here goes to church."

"That's not the point, Charlie!" Fliss's shout echoed in the empty hallway. She glared at Charlie for a long moment before her expression softened. "Look, Leo's messed up big time, but you and I both know that there's no way he wanted to hurt that boy as bad as he did. He's not an ASBO kid; he's had some really horrible stuff happen to him."

"But Mum and Dad know that too, don't they?"

"Of course they do, but they don't see the Leo that you see— that Lila sees—and the social workers have to assume the worst. *Think*, Charlie. Where would he go?"

Charlie shook his head, struggling to grasp whatever it was that Fliss was trying to say. "I don't *know* where he is. I'd tell you if I did, I swear."

"Damn straight, you would." Andy emerged from the kitchen, a mug of tea dwarfed by his large hand. "Which is how I can tell that you don't know jack. Leave him alone, Fliss. He'd say if he knew anything, right? Charlie?"

"Right." Charlie bit his lip, guilt surging through him even though he'd done nothing wrong. Because he did know something that no one else did . . . that he loved Leo, and that perhaps —maybe—that Leo loved him too. "Do you think . . . um—"

"What?" Fliss snapped. "Spit it out."

"*Fliss*," Andy said.

"No, she's onto something." Charlie frantically tried to make sense of the images flashing through his mind. "Give me a minute."

Under the weight of Fliss's glare and Andy's obvious bewilderment, Charlie thought of every bad dream he'd ever watched Leo endure. Every mutter and murmur. Every cry. Every flinch of pain. "The house," he whispered. "Leo and Lila's old house . . . I—I think he's gone there."

"Seriously?" Andy raised an eyebrow. "Why would he go *there*, of all places? There's nothing left of it."

"What do you mean?" Charlie frowned as Fliss stamped on Andy's foot, the message in her furious scowl clear: *shut the fuck up*. "Is that where the fire was?"

Silence. Andy and Fliss stared each other down as new nausea roared in Charlie's gut. Leo never talked about what had brought him and Lila to Kate and Reg's door, and Charlie had assumed that Andy and Fliss were as ignorant as him, but it was obvious now that they both knew something he didn't. "Jesus Christ, you two. Did Mum and Dad tell you what happened? Did you read the file?"

Fliss flushed guiltily and ushered them all down the hall.

"Great," Charlie spat when they were a safe distance from the living room. "So Mum and Dad let you read it, Andy, because you're so much more important than the rest of us, and *you—*" he rounded on Fliss "*—*you just helped yourself, didn't you? Snuck into the office and read the whole thing because you're a nosy bitch—"

"Charlie!" Reg spoke quietly from behind Charlie, but his tone silenced them all as much as any shout ever could. "What's going on out here?"

Charlie pursed his lips, like he could push all the rage back in, even as his arms jittered, desperate to lash out at Fliss, at the wall—anything to ease the fury boiling in his veins. *Is this how Leo feels all the time?* The theory burned Charlie's heart, along with guilt at the certainty that Leo had battered Darren Stroud for giving Charlie pills that he'd *willingly* shoved down his throat.

This is my fault.

"No, it isn't, Charlie," Reg said. "It's no one's fault. Leo has many problems—too many, perhaps, for us to deal with here."

Charlie jumped. *Shit. Did I say that out loud?*

But Fliss shook her head before he could dwell on it much. "No, Dad. You can't kick him out over this. Not after—"

"After *what?*" Charlie cut in, ignoring the fact that he'd inadvertently voiced his worst fear. "Jesus, you take the fucking piss."

Reg held up his hand to silence Charlie and Fliss. "It's not about who knows what, and it never has been. It's about helping Leo as best we can, and right now, that means cooperating with the authorities who are perhaps better equipped to deal with this than we are."

"And by deal with it, you mean take him away," Fliss said bitterly. "Dad, please. Don't let them do that. He's a good kid. And what about Lila? They'll separate them if no other family will take Leo."

"They may be separated anyway if Leo receives a custodial sentence for his attack on that boy." Reg fixed his gaze on Charlie. "And the longer he's gone, the worse it looks for him."

"I don't know where he is," Charlie said.

Fliss stepped in front of him, briefly shielding him from Reg's piercing stare. "But you had an idea, though, didn't you?"

"No."

"Yes, you did." She turned to face Reg. "But we're worried that Leo will freak out if the police turn up there. That he'll run again. Let us go—me, Andy, and Charlie. If he's there, we'll bring him back."

"If he's where?" Reg's tone left nowhere to hide, even for Fliss.

She swallowed hard and lifted her chin. "At the old house . . . where his mum died. Charlie thinks he's gone there."

"Is this true, Charlie?" Reg asked. "Has Leo ever spoken of returning to Swindon before?"

"Um . . . not when he's awake, it's just, um—" Charlie bit his lip. "He talks about the old house in his sleep all the time, like he's worried that he's left something there—or left someone behind."

Something changed in Reg's pale eyes. Concern melted into sadness, and severity turned to the closest to tears that Charlie had ever seen him. "Okay," he said. "If you're going to Swindon,

I'm coming too, which means that someone needs to stay behind and help your mother with Lila while the meeting in there carries on without me."

"I'll stay," Andy said.

Charlie glanced at him in surprise—Andy could never bear to be left out of anything—but Andy shook his head, and looked at Reg.

"This isn't about me," he said. "Or you. We've got to do this as a family, and I reckon Leo needs you right now a lot more than he needs me."

Charlie didn't quite agree. Leo hadn't said much about his Wembley trip with Andy, but it was obvious that he preferred Andy to Reg. That perhaps Reg's presence would be as frightening to him as the police.

But there was nothing else to be done. Reg wouldn't let them go without him, and they *had* to go. Leo had already been alone for far too long.

I'm coming, Leo. I'm coming.

Charlie slouched in the back seat of Reg's beige people-carrier, listening to every word of Reg bollocking Fliss for nosing in Leo's file.

He kind of felt bad for her—kind of, because although he was pissed off that she knew stuff about Leo that he didn't, her snooping had done him a favour. Without it, there was no way that Reg would be having this conversation in front of him, or using it to fill Charlie in on all that he'd missed.

But it wasn't easy listening. Charlie rubbed his sweaty palms together. So far he'd learned that Leo's father was a violent drunk—a story he'd heard before from various siblings who'd passed through the Poulton household—but there was something else lurking behind this tale, a god-awful punch line that Reg and Fliss had yet to reveal.

"How long did the authorities know about the father before the fire?" Fliss asked. "I don't remember what it said in the file. I only skimmed it really, honest."

"That was still a betrayal of trust," Reg said. "I appreciate that you were only so curious because you care about Leo and Lila, but you should know by now that we only keep secrets to protect you and the other children in our care."

"I'm not a child, Dad. You told Andy."

"That's different. Andy has parental responsibility for Charlie if anything happens to us, and as such needed to be informed of exactly what we'd taken on with Leo and Lila. If not for that, we wouldn't have told him either."

Fliss apparently had no argument for that. She huffed and turned her face to the window. "You didn't answer my question."

Reg sighed and activated the windscreen wipers to combat the drizzle that had begun to fall when they'd hit the motorway. "We don't have all the details of the police case before the fire, only what came next, but we were told that a restraining order had been in place for a long time when their father returned to the family home."

"Had he breached it before?"

"I don't know. It's possible that he had, but it wasn't reported, or that the police didn't act on it."

"Idiots," Fliss muttered. "What's the point of a restraining order if no one enforces it?"

"Now, now," Reg counselled. "We can't judge a situation that we know so little about. Ignorance is no excuse for an unfair verdict."

Fliss snorted. "Unfair on who? 'Cause it seems to me that Leo's getting the worst end of it now."

"Maybe so, but he's not blameless in the trouble he finds himself in today. No one made him attack that boy."

"Didn't they?" Fliss shook her head. "Dad, he spent fifteen years with that man. How can we expect him to know any different?"

"He *is* different." The words were out before Charlie could check them. "He's not like that, Fliss. You know he's not."

Fliss glanced over her shoulder. "Of course I do. I told you that at home. I just mean that his behaviour doesn't always match who he is, and that's not his fault, is it, Dad?"

Reg said nothing, his eyes trained on the road. Charlie sat up and put his hand on his shoulder. "Tell me what happened next, then. If you think I'm wrong—that you know Leo better that I do—tell me why."

"You're not wrong. And your mother and I are so proud of the way you've both welcomed Leo and Lila into our home. It's just—" Reg stopped, and Charlie knew that if he hadn't been driving he would've briefly closed his eyes, centred himself, the way he often did when he was about to say something Charlie and Fliss wouldn't like. "Leo is very damaged, Charlie, on the inside as much as his injured arm, and I don't think we truly knew how troubled he was until today."

Charlie wanted to scream. Reg was the master of discretion, but Charlie couldn't handle another nonanswer from him. Not now.

And, finally, Reg seemed to sense that it was time to be frank. "The day of the fire was extremely traumatic for Leo and Lila. They lost their home, and their mother, and both of them continue to suffer the consequences of that fire."

Charlie had figured that Leo's mother was dead. He waited for Reg to go on.

Reg changed lanes and took his cue. "From what I understand, it was breakfast time when Leo's father returned to the family home after a long absence. He got inside somehow, and things turned violent. Leo's mother was killed in a struggle—with a knife, I believe—and the house caught fire in the aftermath, trapping Leo and Lila in a kitchen cupboard where their mother had hidden them."

Charlie took a breath and steeled himself for what was coming next, though he already had a pretty good idea—Lila's weak chest and Leo's ruined arm had seen to that. "Did their father let them go?"

Reg shook his head. "No. Leo had to fight him to try and escape, and then—" He stopped again.

Frustration bubbled over in Charlie's gut. "What, Dad. *What?* Just tell me. I live with his scars too."

But Reg faltered, blinking fiercely at the road, and it was Fliss who turned to face Charlie. "The bastard barred the kitchen door, pulled a table across it so Leo couldn't kick it down. He'd already pocketed the back-door keys."

"He left his kids inside to die?"

"Yes."

Charlie sat back in his seat, numb, save for the roiling beast in his gut. "But they didn't die."

His whisper was for his own sanity as much as the others, and Reg returned to himself and met Charlie's gaze in the rearview mirror. "No, they didn't die, but Leo was badly burned. The flames reached them before they could get through the only window that wasn't locked. The firefighter's report said that Leo's T-shirt was on fire when he fell to the ground outside."

It took a few seconds for Reg's words to sink in, but the imagery reached Charlie first—the fire, the smoke. Lila's terror. Leo's screams as the flames licked his ruined flesh. *Oh, Leo.*

"Stop the car," Charlie gasped. "I'm going to be sick."

FOURTEEN

Leo's secret place was much like the sanctuary Charlie had offered him under the canal bridge, but instead of the lapping water, there were birds rustling the bushes, and squirrels playing in the trees. Before the fire, Leo had spent most of his days in these woods, sitting at the foot of the biggest tree, finding comfort in its broad trunk, even in the rain.

Especially in the rain, and it was raining now, big fat drops that cooled his heated skin. He tried to imagine that the clean water would heal the burning mess on his arm, but reality was too painful for that particular fantasy. And the pain was currently the only thing keeping him awake. Fighting, running, and bunking the train to Swindon had been apparently exhausting, and if not for his arm, he'd be fast asleep.

Wouldn't be the first time you've slept here. Leo closed his eyes and thought of the sticky summer evening when he'd first snatched Lila from her cot and run all the way here, knowing that Dennis couldn't pass the pub without going inside. Wendy had trusted him to keep Lila safe, and he'd stayed here all night with Lila asleep in his arms, waiting for Dennis to go to work the following morning. He repeated the routine a dozen times over the years, before the police had started fetching him home.

Bastards. Hadn't they understood that Leo had had a plan? That if they'd left him alone, he'd have eventually grown up enough to deal with Dennis himself? *They let him kill my mum.*

The rain on Leo's face was suddenly warm. He swiped at his eyes and scrambled to his feet. He didn't cry at the tree. Never had. And he wouldn't cry now. He picked through the dark woods, glad that the path hadn't changed much in his absence. The police had often used dogs to find him and Lila, but Leo needed no help to find his way, just the shape of the trees in the moonlight.

A series of crooked branches led him to the alleyway behind the old house. A brick wall had replaced the rotten fence, and a smart new gate had been fitted at the back. Leo was tempted to scale it, but his arm hurt too much. Instead, he went around the front and squeezed under the tarpaulin that concealed the gap in the scaffolding attached to the house. It was a tight fit, but Leo was slimmer than he'd ever been, and perversely enjoyed the scrape of the bricks against his skin.

The back garden was a boggy mess, ruined first by the clomp of fireman's boots, and then the subsequent building work to make the house safe. Leo's feet squelched in the mud until he came to Wendy's favourite place: the rockery by the shed. Leo ran his hands over the moss-covered stones. In the dark, they felt like velvet, and he smiled. He'd tell Lila about them. She'd like that.

But you're not going to see Lila again.

Leo's smile faded. How had he forgotten? Because if he got away from whoever was likely chasing him by now, he'd never be able to go back to Heyton—not for Lila, or Charlie. *I'll be dead to them.* Perhaps he already was.

He sat on the wet ground, and then lay down as his body

gave up on him. The cold seeped through his torn school shirt and into his bones. His heart wept for Lila, but it cried out for Charlie. Leo had never been cold around him, even walking to school in the frost, their every breath turning to mist and mingling with the smoke of Leo's morning joint.

I was happy then.

I miss him.

Leo closed his eyes. Soon he'd have to move—get up and bunk another train to the end of the world—but, for now, he allowed himself a brief moment with his Charlie-themed dreams that would never come true.

"Leo."

"*Leo.*"

"Dad, he's not waking up."

"Give him a minute, son. It's pretty cold out here."

The voices startled Leo, rousing him from that weird kind of sleep that wasn't really sleep at all—rather a restless doze that teased him with rare moments of blissful oblivion that he wasn't prepared to let go of just yet.

Go away.

But the words stayed inside as the closest voice whispered his name again. *Charlie.* No. He had to be dreaming. Charlie didn't belong in Swindon, or in the bleak future that Leo had resigned himself to, and there was certainly no place for him in the muddy garden of the burned-out house Leo had once called home.

"Leo."

Leo shook his head and flinched away from hands that were definitely *not* Charlie's.

"*Leo.*"

Damn it. Even in his sleep, Leo couldn't ignore Fliss. He opened his eyes a crack. Fliss was glaring down at him. He blinked, sure she'd disappear, but she didn't, and he couldn't deny that her warm palm felt nice on his freezing chest. "Charlie?"

It wasn't what he'd meant to say, but like magic, Charlie was suddenly there, the heat of his touch leaving Fliss in the shade. "I'm here, Leo," he whispered. "But you've got to sit up so we can get you warm, okay? Dad needs to take you home."

Dad. For a long moment, the term meant nothing, but then Reg loomed out of the shadows and reality crashed down on Leo like a frigid wave of despair.

Dad.

Reg.

Heyton.

Fuck.

Leo lurched away from Charlie and Fliss, already mourning the loss of Charlie's addictive touch. "Piss off. You shouldn't be here."

"No, Leo," Fliss said. "*You* shouldn't be here. You should be at home with Lila."

Leo laughed—he couldn't help it—and jabbed a finger at Reg. "That's where you think he'll take me? Home for a cuppa and a game of Uno? Yeah, okay. I know where I'm going, and it's not anywhere with *him*."

"Why not?" Charlie's voice was low and pleading. "Reg has only ever tried to help you. Why would now be any different?"

"He doesn't want to help me. He wants to get rid of me."

Fliss snorted. "So? If you don't want to stay anyway, what's the problem? At least come home and get your stuff. Say good-bye to your sister. 'Cause you don't think social services are going to move her again, do you? When she's doing so well?"

"I don't *want* her to move." Leo hadn't realised how true it was until he said it, and by the sudden light in Fliss's eyes, it appeared that for once, he'd said the right thing. "I don't."

"Why not?" Fliss stepped forward, pulling Charlie behind her before he could protest. "It's because you trust Mum and Dad, isn't it? You know they'll look after her, keep her safe . . . protect her, when you're not around?"

Leo bit his tongue, drawing blood, and absorbing the perverse comfort that came with the bitter, metallic taste. "Kate looks after her."

"Not on her own, she doesn't. And she's not looking after her now—Andy is. Thanks to you, Kate has a house full of social workers and policemen, and you don't want Lila to see all that, do you?"

"Fliss." Reg stepped forward and put a hand on her arm. "That's enough now. We didn't come here to be angry with Leo. He's as upset as the rest of us."

"Is he?"

Fliss's tone dripped with disbelief, and Leo's resolve crumbled a little. Lila and Charlie had his heart to themselves, but he couldn't handle Fliss's scorn, even though what logic he had left warned him that she was playing him—tricking him into admitting that the idea of Lila being with Andy didn't bother him in the slightest.

But it's not Andy that she wants you to trust, is it?

As if on cue, Reg took another step forward, but he didn't move past Fliss; he stopped at Charlie's side and enveloped him in the kind of father-son hug that had always mystified Leo. Reg said something, and Charlie's reply was muffled too, but a soft gasping sound reached Leo, and he belatedly realised that Charlie was crying.

I want to die.

Leo took advantage of Reg's distraction and made a run for the gate.

He's gone.

It took Charlie a moment to process the dark space where Leo's shivering form had just been. Because it hadn't been Leo standing there—pale, cold, and covered in blood, his eyes so vacant he looked like a ghost.

"Dad." He wriggled free of Reg's embrace as Fliss's shout rang out.

"Dad! Leo's gone."

Reg spun around, and for the first time that Charlie could recall, a curse escaped him. "*Shit.* Right. You two go back to the car. Leo's in no state to have gone much distance, and I think I have an idea where he's headed."

"Dad—"

"*No*, Fliss. This has gone far enough."

They all picked their way out of the muddy garden, squeezing past the scaffolding. Charlie's hunch that Leo had returned to his old home had proved true, but he had no idea where Reg thought he might go next, *or* how he'd know. "Dad, I think—"

"Charlie! Go back to the bloody car!"

Charlie flinched and stumbled back into Fliss. She caught him and tugged him away from Reg, who was squinting down the alleyway beside the house. "Come on. Dad'll find him, I promise."

How she could be so sure, Charlie had no clue, but her grip on him left him little choice but to accompany her to the car as Reg disappeared into the night.

Fliss bundled him into the back, then got in the front and started the engine, flooding the car with heat that Charlie barely felt. Didn't want to feel while Leo was still out in the cold. "I don't understand. Where's Dad gone? How can he know where Leo is when he didn't even suspect that he'd be here?"

"I don't know, kid. Perhaps there's something in that damn fucking file that I didn't see."

"Thought you only skimmed it?"

Fliss shrugged. "I did, but I thought I'd absorbed everything that mattered. Serves me right for snooping."

"I'm glad you looked. You'd never have been so nice to Leo and Lila if you hadn't."

"You think?"

Charlie opened his mouth. Shut it again. He didn't think anything. Couldn't. He just wanted Leo.

"So this is your tree, eh?"

If Leo had possessed the energy, he'd have jumped a mile. As it was, he merely gazed at Reg as he loomed out of the darkness, and tried to find the will to berate himself for not running straight for the train station. Damn his tired legs that wouldn't work.

Reg took his coat off and offered it to Leo. "Come on," he said when Leo looked away. "Whatever you do from here isn't going to be any easier if you get hypothermia."

Leo had forgotten about the cold until that moment, but as he stared at the thick anorak Reg was dangling in front of him, it seeped into his bones again, travelling up his spine from where he was sitting at the foot of the tree, and out into his fingers and toes, his lips, his ears. Even his eyelids stung from the bitter wind that had sprung up in the brief few minutes he'd been alone in the woods.

The coat was tempting. Leo felt its warmth oozing out of it, but it was *Reg's* coat. Stuff that.

Eventually, Reg put the coat back on and crouched gingerly on the damp ground for a moment, before giving in and sitting down. He was wearing beige trousers. The thought of him traipsing back to his equally beige car with a damp patch almost made Leo smile.

Almost, because he didn't have the energy for that either. Or to push Reg away when he leaned a fraction closer.

"Your arm's in a bad way," Reg said quietly. "How long has it been like this? Did you hurt it when you were fighting today?"

"Fighting?" For a blissful beat of emptiness, the events of the day eluded Leo, but then, like every memory he tried to ignore, the crunch of the boy's bones against his fist returned, the scent of his blood too. His howls of pain as Leo stamped on his ribs.

Leo shuddered, and Reg's presence beside him faded away as the true reason he'd run all the way to Swindon laid new roots in his soul. Fliss didn't need to trick him into believing that Lila was safe with Kate and Reg—he *knew* that, damn it, even if he didn't like it. It was *him* that she needed protecting from. *Because I'm Dennis.* As playground fights he'd had over the years flashed through his mind like a horror film show reel, it occurred to him that perhaps he always had been Dennis. That a monster lurked inside him too.

"*Leo.*" Reg's palm was scalding on Leo's good arm, and it was clear by his insistent tone that he'd said Leo's name more than once. "Why did you do it?"

"Do what?"

"Any of it. Attack that boy, run away from home . . . I'm not sure I want to know how you got the money for your train ticket."

"I didn't use a ticket. I jumped the barriers."

"Oh . . . well, that's better than helping yourself to Kate's handbag, I suppose."

"I'd never do that."

"Why not?"

Leo blinked. "What?"

"Why wouldn't you steal from Kate?"

"Because—" Leo's brain and tongue failed him. He wouldn't steal from Kate, though he'd helped himself to the purse of his previous foster mothers, but . . . why? What was different about Kate?

"Would you steal from me?"

"I—" Leo shook his head. "No, I wouldn't, but what the fuck does that matter?"

Reg shrugged, like the answer was obvious, and Leo belatedly remembered that Reg would know that he'd lifted cash from his previous homes, because Reg knew every bloody thing about him.

Including where to find him when he didn't want to be found.

"How did you find me?"

"How do you think?" Reg countered.

And Leo's thoughts came full circle again, rinse and repeat. "You saw it in my file."

"Yes, though it didn't say exactly where your favourite tree was—just that you often retreated to the woods when things got bad at home."

"But it's not bad at home, is it? Everything's fucking perfect in your world."

"Nothing's perfect, Leo. But that doesn't mean you can't be happy."

"You're wrong." Leo tipped his head back on the tree trunk and closed his eyes. "I can't be happy, but Lila can. You'll help her, won't you?"

"We want to help you both."

Leo said nothing. If not for Reg's hand on his arm, he'd have found the sleep dancing in front of him and sunk into the oblivion he so desperately craved.

Reg shook him gently. "Leo, we need to make some progress here, even if you don't want to come home. You can't stay here forever."

Leo sighed. Why the hell not? The cold *hurt*, but he'd felt worse pain, and there was no point in moving just yet anyway. Not until Reg left and he could drift to the train station in peace.

Like he'd read Leo's mind, Reg shook him again. "There's nowhere to run from here, son. The police will pick you up the moment you get on a train or a bus."

"I'm not your son."

"I know, and I'm not trying to force you to come with me. I'm simply offering you a lift to wherever you want to go. You owe me nothing, but I can't go home to Kate and Lila and tell them that I left you cold and bleeding in the woods."

Leo opened his eyes and glanced at his arm. In the dark, it was shiny and swollen, the blood darkly vivid, like congealed rust. The sight of it frightened him, shock and horror breaking through the apathy that had kept him on the cold, muddy ground for so long. "It hurts."

Reg nodded. "There's an A and E department a few miles from here. Do you think you can walk that far? Or do you want to come with me now so I can drive you? Whatever you want. It's your decision."

That was bullshit, and they both knew it. The world would end before he left Leo in the woods to fend for himself, because Reg was a universe away from Dennis.

Perspective hit Leo like a train, but he still couldn't find the words to acquiesce. He closed his eyes and thought of Charlie. He'd somehow detached himself from the knowledge that Charlie was likely a stone's throw away, sat in Reg's parked car outside the old house. He'd said good-bye already, even if Charlie hadn't heard him. Could he do it again?

Leo was too tired to decide, and Reg took advantage of his silence by gently tugging him to his feet. "Come on," he said. "I'll drop you at the entrance, if that's honestly what you want. The police will catch up with you eventually, but not through me."

"I don't believe you."

"You don't have to. Just get in the car—I'll do the rest."

"Just get in the car—we'll do the rest." Kate's words so long ago at a house on the other side of the city, echoed in Leo's chaotic brain. He hadn't believed her then, and he didn't believe Reg now, and the hopelessness that overwhelmed him was the same too. His legs wobbled, and Reg's arm was like a snake around his waist.

"Come on," Reg repeated. "You're not going to get very far like this. You don't want our help? To be part of our family? That's fine, but at least let me take you to the hospital to get that arm looked at."

Family. Away from Lila, and maybe Charlie too, the word didn't mean much to Leo, but as Reg's earnest gaze drilled holes in what was left of him, his remaining resolve evaporated. Desperate, he chased it down, fighting his battered body as it slumped into Reg's supporting hold. *No. I don't want to—*

But there was no end to that sentence, because Leo had nothing left. He clung to Reg's waist and buried his face in his chest. *I need help.*

Reg rubbed his back, and then led him slowly through the woods and out into the street Leo had called home for most of his life. The car was parked a little way down the road. Leo stared at it, and wondered why it called to him so strongly. *I don't want to get in the car.* But then one of the back doors opened and a hooded figure climbed out. *Charlie . . . he's here.*

Somehow, Leo had forgotten. He stumbled. Reg caught him again, and called to Charlie. "Get in the car, son. We're coming."

Charlie obeyed. The car engine gunned like an F1 car, and Reg swore. "Damn it, Fliss. How many times have I told her about that heavy right foot, eh?"

Leo turned his face towards Reg as the light from the car illuminated them both. "One of your headlights doesn't work. It hasn't since you first took me and Lila to your house."

"Why didn't you tell me?"

"Because I wanted the police to take you away."

"Why?"

The car pulled up beside them. Leo watched the tyres creep closer to their sodden feet. "Because you had the same shoes as him."

Leo opened the car door and crawled inside. Charlie smiled, and Reg faded away. Fliss too, though Leo was sure he felt her hands on him. He lay down and dropped his head in Charlie's lap, absorbing the warmth radiating from him like a lion in the sun. Charlie had always felt good—magic, even—but now, when there was nothing left of Leo but darkness, Charlie was the sun.

Charlie tangled his fingers in Leo's curls and sighed. "You scare me, Leo."

Leo closed his eyes. *I scare myself.*

FIFTEEN

Charlie paced the landing upstairs, straining his ears for any sign of Reg returning from the Swindon hospital where Leo had been for the last four days. Hypothermia and a blood infection—those things made sense, given the state Leo had been in when they'd found him in his old back garden. Bloodied, freezing, and barely conscious, there had been a split second when Charlie had honestly believed he was dead.

But then Leo had opened his eyes, and Charlie had realised that the cold-induced delirium was only the start of the chaos wreaking havoc in Leo's beautiful soul.

"They won't be long," Fliss said softly from the doorway of Leo's room, where she was entertaining Lila. "Mum texted from the motorway services."

"What about Andy? Where's he?"

"On his way. He'll be here before Mum and Dad."

"Good." Charlie blew out a breath and shoved his shaking hands into his pockets. Leo was due to be discharged the following morning, and until now, Reg had been staying in a Travelodge close to the hospital, but he was coming home today, with Kate, for a family meeting that could only be about one thing: Leo's future.

Lila squeezed past Fliss and trod silently to Charlie's side. She touched his hand.

He glanced down and plastered a smile on his face to sign, *"What's up, little one?"*

The puzzled frown Lila had worn since Leo had abruptly vanished from her life deepened. *"I want Leo."*

Charlie crouched down and gently tugged the pigtails Fliss had plaited into Lila's hair that morning—a concerted effort to keep her occupied while Kate had persuaded the social workers to allow Fliss to care for Lila while she and Reg visited Leo. *"Tomorrow. Leo's still poorly."*

"His arm?"

"Yes." It wasn't exactly a lie. The doctors in Swindon reckoned Leo had been carrying a low-grade infection in his injured arm for months, and that it had got worse slowly enough for no one to notice. Did that explain why Leo had been sick so often? Why his skin had been so clammy and cold when he was upset? Why he'd cried out in the night?

Of course it didn't. The horrors that had brought Leo and Lila into the Poultons' home echoed in Charlie's head every moment he couldn't guard his thoughts, and that would still be there when the infection had cleared.

Lila drifted back to Fliss and the cache of Charlie's art supplies they'd unearthed from under his bed. How Fliss had known they were there, he had no idea, and he didn't much care. Lila could draw on his face with permanent marker if it distracted her from the fact that her brother was still MIA.

The front door opened. Charlie darted to the top of the stairs, but it was only Andy.

Charlie's disappointment apparently showed. Andy grunted and hung his coat over the banister. "Bloody charming.

Drive through rush hour to get here and you haven't even got a brew on."

He stomped down the hall to the kitchen. Charlie hesitated only a moment before following, and reached Andy's side just as he was tossing teabags into the pot. "What do you know?"

Unflappable as ever, Andy filled the kettle with water from the tap. "About what?"

"About Leo. Are they sending him away? Are the police going to take him? Will he go to prison? What about—"

Andy held up a hand. "Whoa. One thing at a time."

"*Tell* me." Charlie worked his jaw. "It's not fair that I'm always the last to know."

"Yeah, well. Life isn't fair, squirt, and I can't fix it this time. All I can tell you is that Ma and Pa are doing everything they can for Leo, but you know that already, if you've got any sense."

"That doesn't tell me anything."

"Doesn't it? Do you think Dad would stay in a pissy Travelodge for days for a kid he was turfing back into the system?"

"He's never *turfed* anyone anywhere."

"Exactly. So why are you doubting him now? He's only ever let kids go who he can't help. Who *we* can't help. Leo's no different."

Charlie scowled, because Andy was wrong about that. Leo *was* different. "What about the police?"

Andy shrugged and poured boiling water into the chipped teapot. "The school reported the incident, so police will want to talk to Leo, but whether he's charged or not, depends on the kid."

"On Darren bloody Stroud?"

"If that's the name of the kid whose ribs Leo kicked in, yes. If he presses charges, then Leo's in a lot of trouble, even with Dad arguing for diminished responsibility."

"What does that mean?"

"That Leo isn't—or wasn't, at the time—mentally well enough to know what he was doing. It's a long shot, but given his history, it's pretty plausible."

"Darren Stroud doesn't deserve any sympathy. He booted seven bells of shite out of a year nine last term."

Andy sighed. "That doesn't make what Leo did okay. Besides, Leo has to live with what he's done, and he might find that easier if he's properly punished. Do you really want to add a shedload of guilt onto all the crap he's already carrying?"

Charlie knew that Andy was right. Darren Stroud was a prat who had no business chucking eggs at teachers' cars, looking up girls' skirts, and offering idiots like Charlie pills in the local park, but what Leo had done to him had hurt everyone —and perhaps hurt Leo most of all. "Do you think they'll let him come home?"

"Who? Ma and Pa, or social services?"

"Everyone, I guess."

"I honestly don't know, mate. It's not just Leo they have to consider—there's you, and Lila, and any other kid they might take in the future."

"They can't separate Leo and Lila."

"Can so, especially if they think that he's dangerous . . . that she'd be better off without him."

Charlie took Andy's words like a punch to the gut. "You don't think that, do you?"

Andy dumped sugar into a stained Mr. Men mug and mechanically stirred his tea. Then he sighed again. "I want to believe the worst, because then the answer is obvious—he's gotta go. But I can't bring myself to think that way, because the Leo I see with that little girl upstairs isn't the boy battering kids in the playground."

"He's not a monster."

"I know, so that's exactly what I'm going to say when Ma

and Pa come home. They've probably made up their minds already, but we can still speak for Leo, eh? Seeing as he's not here to speak for himself."

The reminder of Leo's absence lanced Charlie's heart, but as far as the family meeting was concerned, he was glad of it. There was nothing worse than hashing out the future of a messed-up kid all the while aware that they were likely camped on the stairs, listening to every word.

A car pulled up on the drive. Charlie's stomach flip-flopped as the unmistakable sound of Kate crunching the gearbox reached him.

It's time.

Reg and Kate came inside, Reg heading straight for the table, Kate to the kitchen, no doubt to rustle up something sweet to soften the blow of whatever she had to say.

But no amount of her signature chocolate shortbread would lessen the pain of losing Leo. And it was Lila who danced through Charlie's mind as he took his seat. She needed Leo more than anyone, and Charlie wasn't going to let anyone take him from her.

Not even Leo.

Kate breezed into the room and set a plate on the table just as Fliss appeared with Lila in tow. Kate knelt in front of Lila and signed, *"iPad? I have milk and biscuits for you."*

Lila stopped in the doorway, scanning the room. *"Where's Leo?"*

"Hospital."

"Home tomorrow?"

Kate glanced briefly at Reg, who gave a subtle nod. *"Maybe,"* Kate signed. *"If he's well enough."*

The half answer was apparently enough for Lila. She drifted to the couch and picked up the iPad from the coffee table. Fliss took her a plate of biscuits and a glass of milk, and it wasn't long before she was engrossed in her game.

"Sit down, everyone," Reg said. "The sooner we get this done, the better."

"For who?" Fliss muttered.

"For all of us," Kate said sharply. "This isn't the time for snide comments."

Fliss flushed and, for once, didn't retaliate. And Charlie was grateful. There was enough to talk about without Fliss losing her rag.

"So . . ." Reg started. "It's been a hell of a week, but before we get down to the nitty-gritty, you probably all want to know how Leo is?"

"Damn right," Andy said. "Tell us everything you can."

"I'll tell you it all." Reg stared directly at Charlie. "Leo doesn't want to hide anything."

"He said that? To you?"

Charlie couldn't contain his shock, and Reg smiled a tiny wry smile. "You'd be surprised what Leo and I have talked about these last few days. There's not much else to do on a hospital ward, even a children's one, but yes . . . he wants you all to know what we know, so you can make your own judgements."

"Is he feeling better?" Fliss asked. "He looked like death the last time I saw him."

Charlie could only nod and fight against the image of Reg half dragging Leo from his arms and carrying him into the hospital. There'd been nothing behind Leo's vacant stare. Nothing behind the chill of his freezing skin. Charlie had honestly believed he'd never see him again, and he'd cried on Fliss's shoulder the whole way home.

"Leo's still poorly," Kate said, casting a glance at Lila. "The antibiotics he was given for his arm have made him quite sick.

But he's on the mend, physically, and he'll be ready to be discharged tomorrow."

Physically. The word resonated more than any other Kate had ever uttered at a family meeting. Charlie sat up straighter in his seat, and so did Fliss. Andy poured himself another mug of tea, as though bracing himself, and asked the question Charlie couldn't articulate.

"So his arm's gonna be okay. What about the rest of it? Are we talking PTSD, or some shit? Something else?"

"You're spot on, actually," Reg said. "Which has come as a relief to Kate and I. A diagnosis is a good starting point for recovery, and the hospital psychiatrist agrees that there's much that can be done to help Leo."

"Done by who?" Charlie wanted to slap his hands over his mouth and shove the words back in, because he wasn't ready for Reg's gentle headshake, or the tearful regret in Kate's eyes. But he fought the urge to flee the room and raised his chin in defiance, digging in to fight in Leo's corner. "*Who's* going to help him, Dad? Because you promised him we would."

"I did, Charlie, but things have changed since then. Leo has deteriorated despite the efforts we've all made to care for him."

"But you didn't know what was wrong with him," Fliss said. "Surely it will be easier now."

"Nothing we do from here is going to be easy." Kate leaned forward, her hands reaching out for all of them. "But—" her gaze flickered to Reg before she seemed to make a decision. "Reg and I have decided that we'd like to bring Leo home tomorrow. What do you all think?"

"That you should've said that in the first place." Fliss spoke before Charlie could. "We love Leo. There's no way that any of us would've agreed to you doing anything else. Right, guys?"

She looked to Andy and Charlie, who both nodded.

"Damn straight," Andy said. "We've come this far, though I don't live here, so Charlie should speak before me."

Abruptly, all eyes were on Charlie. He gulped and nodded again, fervently this time, like the felt dog Andy had in the back of his car. "Leo *needs* to come home, Mum. Where else would he go?"

They all knew the answer to that: emergency foster care or a group home. Kate blanched and shook her head. "If we can agree, we'll bring him back tomorrow, but Charlie, you spend a lot of time with Leo, so it's only fair that we warn you that his recovery might prove disruptive."

Charlie rolled his eyes, couldn't help it. "Mum, he already keeps me up half the night with his nightmares and insomnia, and I don't care. I love him, okay? And I want him to come home."

He pushed his chair back and finally gave in to the urge to escape to his bedroom. He'd spent days anticipating this conversation, and the relief of it being over was too much. Leo was coming home, and Charlie couldn't bloody wait.

Shame Fliss felt the need to invade his much-needed privacy mere moments after he'd shut his bedroom door.

"You know you have to tell them, don't you?"

"Tell who what?"

Fliss rolled her eyes and leaned on the closed door. "Don't give me that nonsense. I've kept quiet until now because it's none of my business, but PTSD is serious, Charlie. Mum and Dad need to know everything if they're going to help Leo— including about the little cuddle party you two have got going on. What if it goes tits up, Leo gets upset, and they don't know why?"

"I don't know what you're on about."

"Liar."

"I *don't*," Charlie insisted, opening his wardrobe to hide the flush burning his cheeks.

"Want me to spell it out?"

"Piss off." Charlie grabbed a T-shirt and pulled the one he was wearing over his head, replacing it with the clean one. "Can't you annoy Andy for a while instead of me? It must be his turn."

"Andy isn't wearing Leo's clothes."

Damn. Charlie looked down at the T-shirt he'd mindlessly slipped on. It *was* Leo's. Of course it was. "What do you want from me? To pay you to shut the hell up? To keep your mouth shut?"

"What do you think this is? A bloody soap opera?" Fliss let out an exasperated sigh. "Charlie, I'm not trying to ruin your life. I'm just warning you that Mum and Dad need to know that you and Leo are, uh, seeing each other. They could get in a lot of trouble if social services found out first. And Leo needs us, remember? How would you feel if they took him away?"

Of all the things Charlie had spent the last few days worrying about, never once had he considered that. "They couldn't do that, could they?"

"They could if they thought you and Leo were up to anything inappropriate while you were sneaking across the landing every night."

The fading flush in Charlie cheeks returned full force, incinerating his skin from within. "We haven't done anything."

Fliss shrugged. "Doesn't matter if you have. It's the suspicion that will screw things up."

"But—" Charlie's brain worked overtime, trying to push aside the embarrassment burning a path through every vein. "If I tell Mum and Dad, they won't let Leo come home."

"Yes, they will."

"No, they won't. He'll have nowhere to sleep if they won't let him sleep so close to my room anymore."

"He will if I move out. He can have my room."

"But—"

"Stop saying *but*. You sound like a moron."

"But—" Charlie searched for a coherent sentence to prove Fliss wrong "—where would you go?"

"Andy has a spare room."

"You hate Andy's house."

"Only because it smells of stale garlic. He's got a wicked stereo system, and he works early shifts six days a week. I'd never see him."

But . . . Charlie stopped himself just in time and allowed Fliss's bombshell to take root in his whirling mind. His head told him that Fliss leaving home would be the best thing in the world —Christ, how many times had he wished her away?—but his heart was heavy. For better or worse, Fliss was his sister, and life without her was unthinkable. "I don't want you to move out."

"Why not? It's not like it wouldn't have happened eventually anyway."

"Mum won't let you."

"I'm twenty, Charlie. Not fifteen."

Fliss had a point, and the more Charlie thought about it, the more her moving in with Andy made sense. He was always moaning that he didn't like living alone—or leaving his delinquent cat to its own devices when he was out. If Kate and Reg could live with Charlie and Leo residing on separate floors of the house, Fliss's solution was perfect.

The only problem was that it was built on an assumption that Charlie had no right to make. Charlie's own misgivings about confessing to Kate and Reg aside, he had no idea how Leo would feel about it. *And, duh, it's not like he ever agreed to be your bloody boyfriend. Get real, loser.*

Charlie tried to silence the pessimistic devil on his shoulder, but it was hard, and even without the bullshit that came with that, there was something else—something that mattered more than anything: *Leo.*

Leo was still so unwell, and revealing his sexuality alongside Charlie's, to a family he still barely knew, probably wasn't high on his list of priorities. If it was on there at all.

Charlie shook his head slowly, trying to clear it. "Please don't tell Mum and Dad."

"I'm not going to. You are."

"I can't. Not without talking to Leo first. He might not want to be with me when he comes home anyway."

Fliss scoffed. "Bollocks. That kid's as crazy about you as you are about him. Which is why you need to handle this properly. I'm trying to help you, Charlie. Not stuff it up for you."

"Why?"

"Because I want everyone to be happy. Makes my life easier."

"Nothing about this is easy." Charlie echoed Kate's earlier words with little conscious thought and dropped his head into his hands. Perhaps Fliss was right and he *did* need to tell Kate and Reg about him and Leo, but with Leo so poorly, and his absence a giant crater in Charlie's soul, where the hell would he start?

Mum, Dad, I've got something to tell you . . .

SIXTEEN

Leo let his head loll against the car window, only half listening to Reg as he spoke about what would happen when they finally got home. It was as much as his tired brain would allow, especially after the doctor had given him a pill to *"ward off any anxiety you may have about leaving the hospital."*

The pill had done little to ease the tense knot in his chest, but Leo couldn't deny that the drowsy buzz behind his eyes felt good—soothing—and the cool glass against his aching head felt even better.

"I don't know if you'll be able to go back to school anytime soon," Reg said.

"Hmm?" Leo lifted his head.

Reg smiled slightly, before his expression became characteristically grave again. "I'm talking about school, Leo. It's important."

School was the last thing on Leo's mind, but he'd come to realise in recent days that listening to Reg talk about boring stuff that didn't matter was kind of nice. Like watching a film you'd seen a hundred times over. "Did I get expelled?"

"The school hasn't decided what to do with you yet."

"What about the police?"

"Darren Stroud's family decided not to press charges, but I'd imagine the police will want to talk to you anyway." Reg's lips pressed into a thin line. Leo sat up straighter. Until now, Reg had given little indication of his feelings on what Leo had done to Darren Stroud. Was that about to change?

A flicker of fear dampened the medication-mellowed fire in his gut, but then he remembered the many hours he'd lost to Reg's voice over the last few days and the flicker went away. If Reg was angry, it was only because he cared. *You're family, Leo. Whatever happens, we'll take care of you.*

It was nothing that Reg hadn't said from the start, and perhaps it was the medication, but somehow, Leo had come to believe him. "What are you pissed off about?" Leo asked. "Do you want them to press charges so I get what I deserve?"

"It's not for me to decide what you deserve, but no . . . it's not that I want you to be prosecuted. I'm more concerned with the fact that the other boy's parents weren't that interested in what had happened to their son. I shouldn't tell you this, but the school had to accompany him to the hospital and the police brought him home."

Guilt was an emotion that Leo was familiar with, though he found it hard to apply to Darren Stroud, especially when he thought of Charlie—beautiful, innocent Charlie, dancing through Heyton, off his tits on dodgy pills.

Dennis's face flashed into Leo's mind, stronger and clearer than even Charlie's. Leo shuddered and closed his eyes. The doctors at the hospital had told him that the PTSD was probably in part responsible for what he'd done to Darren Stroud, but all the pills in the world couldn't convince him that he wasn't a fistfight away from becoming Dennis.

"*Leo.*" Reg's voice was insistent. "Come on, now. If the police pursue a case, it's unlikely that you'd serve a custodial sentence. It's more likely that a judge would insist on you getting the treatment you'll be having anyway."

"Treatment?"

"Treatment, therapy, assistance. It's all semantics, really."

"I literally have no idea what you're on about."

Reg smiled properly this time. "They're just words, son. All that matters now is getting you better, but you know that most of that will fall on you, don't you? No one can feel things for you, which is a shame."

"Is it?"

"Well, yes and no. I dread to think how many children Kate would have taken the pain and suffering from, if it were possible."

"I'd do it for Lila."

"I know you would. And so will she when she's old enough to process everything you've both been through."

Leo absorbed Reg's words with a nod and then let his head return to its love affair with the window. It was odd to be communicating so easily with Reg when he'd spent so long avoiding him, but the shift between them had happened sometime between Leo kicking in Darren Stroud and waking up in a horribly familiar hospital, and he was too tired to fight it. Reg was here, and so was Leo, and apparently that wasn't changing anytime soon.

Sometime later, Leo woke up to Reg gently shaking him.

"We're home, son."

Son. That shit was still annoying. *Damn it, just call me Leo.* But the prospect of seeing Lila—and Charlie—distracted Leo from even scowling in Reg's direction. He rubbed his face and pushed his matted curls from his forehead, hoping his glassy eyes and haggard appearance wouldn't frighten Lila. "Do I look okay?"

"Of course you do, though I reckon Kate will try and feed you the moment you get in." Reg got out of the car and was somehow at Leo's door in the blink of an eye. He opened it, then helped Leo out before he could protest. "When you get inside, go wherever you're most comfortable. We'll bring Lila to you if she's not already there."

But Reg's offer proved unnecessary, because Lila was exactly where Leo knew she would be—perched on the living room windowsill, counting his steps until he reached her.

He scooped her down with his good arm and embraced her as tightly as he could manage. Whispered words were on his lips, even though she'd never hear them. "I'm here, kiddo. I'm sorry."

Lila squeezed him fiercely, then pulled away, her face marred by the innocent confusion Leo's heart could never take. *"Are you okay?"* she signed.

"I am now."

"I'm hungry."

"What's new?"

There was movement behind them. Leo whirled around, still clutching Lila, and disappointment hit him like a punch to the gut as Kate chanced a hopeful smile with her plate of sandwiches that she set on the coffee table.

"I've brought you lunch," she signed to Lila.

"Where's Charlie?" Leo blurted, and then wanted to smack himself as something inscrutable flickered in Kate's eyes.

"He's at school," she said. "It's Monday, remember?"

Leo had stopped caring what day of the week it was a long time ago. School often felt like the bane of his life, but before Charlie, weekends had brought a nightmare all of their own. *But it's not like that anymore. You trust Reg now, don't you?*

Did he? *Do I?*

Reg came into the living room. He smiled at Lila, and then met Leo's eyes with a steady gaze that stirred nothing in Leo—demanded nothing. A kindly stare that reminded him only of his empty stomach.

Leo stepped forward and took a sandwich from the plate. "Thank you."

"No problem," Kate said, her features brightening with a cautious delight that made Leo wonder what sort of git he'd been the last time she'd seen him. "I'll fetch some drinks, then we'll leave you to it."

And of course she made good on her promise. Leo was coming to realise that she and Reg always did.

Later that afternoon, after *way* too many games of Mouse Trap and Uno, Leo fell asleep on the couch while Lila watched *Despicable Me* on the iPad. Nasty dreams had plagued him for years, but the antibiotic-induced illusions weren't so bad. He was quite happily playing football with duck-billed unicorns when Kate woke him sometime later.

"Teatime," she said. "And medicine time."

She dropped an antibiotic into his palm, along with the final dose of pills from the psychiatrist. Somehow, Reg had wangled him a stay of execution on any more until "other options" had been explored, whatever that meant.

Leo swallowed the pills, knowing he'd miss the numbing buzz of the sedative, and sat up slowly, flexing his tender arm, loosening the muscles that had stiffened while he slept. He searched automatically for Lila. She was already at the table, eagerly filling her plate in a way that warmed Leo from the inside out. *This is her home.* And then guilt hit him hard, like it had so many times since his faculties had returned to him in the hospital. Reg had promised him that whatever happened, he and Kate would always look after Lila, but that didn't make up for how close Leo had come to abruptly exiting her life.

"Come on, love," Kate prompted. "Do you need a hand up?"

"No, thanks." Leo could stand, and he did, with barely a wobble as he scanned the room once more, for Charlie this time, an odd mixture of anticipation and nerves churning in his stomach.

But Charlie was nowhere in sight, and pride kept Leo from asking for him again as he drifted to the table. He took his seat next to Lila and stared at a groove in the wood as Kate bustled around with lasagne and garlic bread. Fliss appeared opposite, ignoring him entirely, which was strangely comforting. But still no Charlie.

Come on, come on. Leo counted the cherry tomatoes in the salad until heated fingers finally grazed his good wrist and Charlie dropped into the seat beside him.

"Hi."

Leo swallowed thickly. "Hi."

"Okay?"

"Um . . . yeah?"

"Good, 'cause you look like shit."

"Language, Charlie," Reg cautioned, but there was a smile in his eyes that lightened the air.

Leo smiled too, and for a fleeting moment, the world seemed as right as it could be.

Somehow, he made it through dinner without falling into Charlie's arms. When it was over, he picked up the nearest plate, eager to get the table cleared as quickly as possible.

Fliss pried it from his tingling fingers. "I've got this. Mum's bathing Lila. Go upstairs and rest."

Leo didn't need telling twice, he glanced at Charlie and then fled his room, praying Charlie would follow.

His head had barely touched his pillow when Charlie slipped through the door and shut it firmly behind him. Leo started to sit up, but Charlie reached him before he'd got far, and pushed him back down.

"Stay. Mum says you need to rest."

"I've been asleep all afternoon."

"Humour me. I had a dream last night that you'd killed yourself."

A chill ran through Leo. "I wouldn't do that."

"Promise."

"What?"

"*Promise.*" Charlie sat on the edge of the bed, leaned over, and pressed his forehead to Leo's. "I know you feel bad, Leo—like, really bad—but you can get better. Dad said lots of people recover from PTSD."

"But—"

"But nothing. None of this is your fault."

"It is. I hurt that dickhead who gave you those pills."

"So? You weren't in your right mind. Uh, Dad told me what happened to your mum—" Charlie held up his hand as Leo took a breath to speak. "It's okay. I know you don't want to talk about it. That's cool, and it always will be. Just don't let what happened destroy you, Leo. You're worth more than that."

He got up as abruptly as he had sat down, and retreated to his own room. Leo watched him undress in the window and became lost in his long limbs and flawless skin. He felt calmer now than he had in weeks, perhaps months, or even years, but the ability to share that with Charlie eluded him. With his tongue stuck to the roof of his mouth, he rolled over and stared at the wall until sleep claimed him again.

It was pitch-dark when slender arms slipped around his

waist from behind, the bulb in his lamp apparently dead. But Leo paid the blackness no heed as a slender form pressed up against him, treating his skin to the best kind of fire. Leo kept his eyes closed and leaned back into the healing warmth. "Charlie?"

His voice was croaky and hoarse, and his throat hurt. Charlie tugged him onto his back and then supported his head while he pressed a bottle of water to Leo's lips. "Mum said the sedatives made your mouth dry."

And the rest. Leo swallowed the water. "Kate and Reg say a lot, eh?"

"Only when it matters."

Leo had no answer to that. He lay back down, facing Charlie this time, and Charlie mirrored his pose. "I missed you."

Charlie smiled, his eyes gleaming in the dark. "I missed you too."

"Yeah? Even though I'm a nutter?"

"Don't say that. It's not true. You'd be more crazy if you'd survived all you have without being affected by it."

A nurse in the hospital had said that to Leo. He'd vaguely recognised her, and in a brief moment of coherent thought had wondered if she'd treated him before. After all, it had been far from the first time he'd found himself in Swindon Hospital. "Do you think I'll get better?"

"I think you can . . . if you try really hard. You'll have to have loads of counselling and stuff, but Kate and Reg are good with things like that. Fliss used to go to a therapist."

"Fliss did? What was it? Anger management?"

Charlie snorted. "You'd think. I'm not sure what it was for, just that she went, and after a while, she stopped crying in the night . . . like you do."

Leo didn't have the strength to look away. He held Charlie's gaze and pushed aside the shame that came with knowing his messed-up dreams had disturbed Charlie too.

Charlie's fingers wrapped around his wrist, his thumb pressed into his pulse point. "I need to talk to you about something."

SEVENTEEN

"I need to talk to you about something . . ."

The stricken look on Leo's face was more than Charlie could take. He wrapped his arms around Leo and held him as tight as he dared. "It's nothing bad—at least, I don't think it is. If it all works out, nothing has to change."

Leo spoke.

Charlie realised he was muffling him and reluctantly loosened his hold. "Sorry."

Leo blinked, his hair a riot that would've been funny if the stampeding tattoo of Charlie's heart wasn't so distracting. Leo rubbed his eyes and fumbled for Charlie's hands, squeezing them in a death grip. "I hate it when someone tells me shit that they don't think is bad. They're always wrong."

"I might be wrong." Charlie bit his lip. "But it's something that has to happen even if I am, so—"

"*Charlie*, what is it? You're killing me here."

Leo rarely interrupted anyone unless he was angry—and lost. But he didn't seem to be either now. His eyes were as bright has Charlie had ever seen them, his skin warm against Charlie's.

His strong fingers wrapped around Charlie's own gave

Charlie courage. "We need to tell Mum and Dad about—uh—about you and me."

"Me and you?"

"Yes. Fliss knows, and if we don't tell them, she will."

"Why would she do that?"

That Leo hadn't scoffed at the idea that Fliss had anything to tell stirred an odd heat in Charlie's veins. He absorbed it, welcomed it, and squeezed Leo's even tighter. "She said Mum and Dad will get in trouble if social services find out, especially as our rooms are so close together, and I think she's right."

"But—" Leo stopped and shook his head slightly. "But we haven't done anything wrong."

"I know, but there's rules and stuff. Fliss said that if we don't come clean now and let Mum and Dad handle it properly, social services might find out and remove one of us."

"Remove me, you mean. I'm the troublemaker, and they can't touch you regardless. You're adopted, remember?" Leo fell back on his pillows and stared at the ceiling, his expression unreadable. "Kate and Reg will probably get rid of me anyway when they find out about this."

"Why would you think that?"

"Obvious, ain't it? I've messed everything up—for you, for them, for Lila. Do you all good if I fucked off somewhere else."

Anger flared in Charlie before he could check it. He moved fast and covered Leo's body with his own, pressing their foreheads together hard enough to make his skull throb. "Don't say that."

"But—"

"*Don't.*"

Leo shivered. His fear was hard to swallow, but Charlie would take it over his habitual apathy any day of the week. Besides, lying over Leo like this, their legs, hips, and chests moulded together, was enough to distract him from just about any emotion Leo could throw at him.

He drew back from the game of mercy he'd been playing with Leo's skull. "It's going to be okay. Fliss said you can have her room if Mum and Dad want us farther apart—and that if we tell them now, it should be enough for them to deal with social services. It's if we get caught that there'll be trouble, especially while we're both fifteen."

Leo's eyes blazed, and Charlie thought for a moment that he would kiss him, but then Leo sighed, and the scorching heat between them passed, chased away by a ruthless reality that couldn't be ignored. "I didn't think you were ready to tell anyone you're gay."

Gay. Despite being certain of his sexuality for as long as he could remember, the word still hit Charlie like a train. Kate and Reg would barely blink, he was sure of it—his friends too— but what about the rest of the world? Oh god, what about *school?*

Leo touched Charlie's face, the featherlight trail of his fingertips along Charlie's jaw more grounding than anything he could have said. "Just because you tell your parents, doesn't mean anyone else has to know."

"Is that what you want? To keep it a secret? Because if people find out about us, they'll know you're gay too."

Duh, obvious much? But if Leo thought Charlie was as daft as he sounded, it didn't show. He merely shrugged. "I don't care who knows about me. Only reason I don't talk about it is because it's no one's business. Besides, it's not like my reputation around here isn't already fucked."

Leo had a point, and Charlie couldn't imagine that anyone at school would mess with him after what he'd done to Darren Stroud. Wouldn't stop them coming after Charlie, though—

"Stop it." It was Leo's turn to press his forehead into Charlie's. "No one has to know, okay? Not if you don't want them to. Nothing has to change. You said it yourself."

"Did I?"

"Yes, when you were rambling about having something to tell me. I thought I was about to get dumped."

"Oh . . . well, you're not, if that's any consolation."

"It is." A ghost of a grin warmed Leo's features. "So, anyway . . ."

"What?"

"I'm just thinking that if I move to Fliss's room, we won't be able to do this anymore."

"'This'?"

And then it clicked, and the way they were lying made itself known again. Charlie flushed and ducked his head, trying to ignore the yearning desire in every part of his body to be as close to Leo as possible. But it was no good. Leo was right. Once they'd told Kate and Reg, their nights of creeping across the landing to snuggle in bed together were over.

The need to make the most of their freedom was abruptly overwhelming—for Leo too, apparently, as he rose up to meet Charlie's kiss. Their lips met, sweetly at first, but then harder as the heat they'd lived with for so long took hold.

Leo rolled them, pressing Charlie's back into the mattress, and holding him there with his weight. Charlie gasped and dug his fingers into Leo's back, fisting his T-shirt, and wondered if he dared stake a claim on the skin that lay beneath.

I want to touch him.

I need to touch him.

Resolved, Charlie fought Leo for dominance, and won, rolling them again, and tugging at Leo's T-shirt until Leo gave in and pulled it over his head.

Oh God.

Charlie had seen Leo shirtless before on the rare occasions

that Leo had changed his T-shirt in Charlie's room, but now, with him so close, Charlie tasting the sweet scent of his smooth skin, it was almost too much.

Almost, because nothing was going to stop Charlie laying his palm on Leo's chest and counting the beats of his thudding heart.

"I love it when you do that to my wrist," Leo whispered. "It feels like you catch the fear and push it all away."

If only. Charlie would take every terror Leo had endured if such a thing were possible. "Kiss me, Leo."

Leo obliged, and returned the favour of stripping Charlie of his T-shirt. Their bare chests touched and the stars exploded.

It was nearly dawn and neither of them had slept. Charlie lay with Leo's head in his lap and ran his fingers through Leo's hair. "Are you okay?"

Leo hummed lazily. "Yeah. Are you?"

"Yeah."

They didn't speak again for a long while. Charlie amused himself with Leo's crazy hair, and then, when he'd run out of curls to wrap around his fingers, turned his attention to Leo's arm.

The sight of it made him want to wrap Leo in his arms and never let go, but they'd done that already, and their reality seemed all the more real. Leo's arm was just the start of his wounds, and for him to stand any chance of healing, their confession needed to happen as soon as possible.

"Stop staring at it."

It was a phrase Leo had thrown at Charlie before, but there was no bitterness in his tone now, only a gentle admonishment that stirred Charlie's soul. "Did it hurt when it happened?"

"When it was burning?"

"Um, yeah . . . I suppose."

Leo shrugged, and his sleepy eyes flickered with an emotion Charlie couldn't quite decipher. "It didn't hurt at the time, or even when I first saw it. Adrenaline kept me moving until Lila was safe, and then I hit my head falling out of the window. At least, that's what they said when I told them that I couldn't feel it."

"You couldn't feel it at all?"

"Nope. Not until I got to the burn unit at the hospital and they started messing around with it. I screamed the bloody place down then."

Charlie shuddered, hardly able to imagine the pain behind the burned wreck of Leo's arm without screaming himself. "I bet you waited for Lila to be taken care of before you showed any pain."

"Not on purpose. I lost my shit as soon as I felt it."

Charlie knew he was right, though. There was much he still didn't know about Leo, but his protection of his little sister was absolute. And now Charlie had to protect him. "I'm going to speak to Dad in the morning."

"Uh-huh."

Leo's tone gave nothing away. Charlie held Leo's head up and slid down the bed. "Do you want to come with me? I can do it by myself if—"

"Charlie, I'm coming with you."

"You are?"

"Course I am. You think I'd let you do it on your own?"

Charlie hadn't really thought about it. In the hours he'd spent tonight simply holding Leo, he'd imagined only a world where they could always be like this—free and happy, the only complication the threat of the rising sun. "I'd like you to come," he said. "And it will be easier. Mum and Dad will want to hear it from you anyway. They won't just take my word for it."

Leo grunted and rolled onto his stomach, his face smushed against Charlie's ribs. He was clearly fading, and it wouldn't be long before he fell asleep.

Charlie didn't have that luxury. Reg would be up soon, and he needed to be back in his own bed by then. But there was one thing he needed to know before he tore himself from Leo's arms. "Leo?"

"Yeah?"

"Look at me."

Leo raised his head, squinting into the faint light that was beginning to filter through the open curtains. "What is it?"

Charlie chewed on his lip until he tasted blood. Leo swiped at it with his thumb. "Come on. Just say it. Can't be worse than the shit we've already been through."

And there it was—the glimmer of hope Charlie so desperately needed every time he met Leo's eyes. "Do you honestly believe that? That it's all going to be okay . . . in the end?"

Leo held Charlie's gaze for a long moment before he slowly nodded. "I believe it *can* be, if I want it enough."

"Do you? Do you want it enough?"

Leo smiled tiredly, his eyes barely open. "Course I do, mate. I want it all."

EIGHTEEN

Six months later . . .

"Slow breaths, Leo." Reg's hand was warm on Leo's shoulder. "You're not on trial, remember? Just answer the questions to the best of your ability. No one's asking any more of you."

"You're not on trial . . ."

Maybe not, but if the police hadn't walked away from what he'd done to Darren Stroud last winter, he probably would've been by now.

Don't think about that.

Leo shoved his hands in the pockets of his jeans. Kate had wanted him to wear his school trousers, but Reg had dissuaded her: *"Let him be comfortable, love."* After all, with Leo's evidence being prerecorded, it wasn't like many people would see him today—just the judge and the barrister for the prosecution.

"He won't be able to see you, Leo. I promise."

Leo hadn't believed the lawyers, but Reg had only had to tell him once.

He won't see me.

Leo didn't know much, but of that, he was certain.

"Are you ready?" This time, it was Carol, the social worker, who spoke—a kind woman who wore her hair in long plaits and who had become Leo's loudest champion outside of the Poulton family.

Leo nodded and steeled himself. Dennis was far away in his prison cell, but opening the wounds Leo had fought so hard to heal still wasn't going to be easy. Already, his heart was skipping beats, his skin burning with the phantom fire that all the love in the world had never entirely extinguished. He pointed to the door at the end of the stark corridor. "In there?"

Carol nodded. "Let's go."

Like most things Leo found himself afraid of in his new life, the anticipation of giving evidence against Dennis turned out to be worse than the actual event. The questions he was asked were no worse than he'd expected, and no one argued with his answers.

And when he closed his eyes and hid his face, they stopped —at least until he was ready for them to continue.

When it was over, Leo emerged from the small, airless room to find Reg waiting for him at the nearest exit.

"Let's get out of here," Reg said. "You tell me how it went on the way back to the car. If you want to, that is. It's okay if you don't."

Leo waved good-bye to Carol and followed Reg out of the court building. "You wouldn't ask me anything if I said I didn't want to tell you?"

Reg smiled wryly. "You are allowed to keep some things to yourself."

Leo grunted, because the way things had changed at home in recent months had left him little of the privacy he desperately craved, and Reg knew it. Not that Leo was going to complain about moving into Fliss's light and airy loft bedroom, even if it did mean that he and Charlie rarely got the chance to be truly alone. The shadows were bright in the attic, and Leo slept among them like he'd never slept before.

They reached the car. Leo slid into the passenger seat and retrieved his Arsenal snapback cap from the back seat to jam on his head. "Are we going home now?"

Reg smiled and handed over the phone he'd taken off Leo before they'd gone inside the court building. "I think you have a call to make first. I asked the school to let Charlie answer his phone at lunchtime. It's quarter to one. If you ring now, you'll catch him."

Charlie. Leo had fought hard to keep Charlie from his thoughts since they'd parted at breakfast that morning, because Charlie was beautiful, and pure, and deserved better than to share Leo's headspace with Dennis.

But that was over now. Leo's evidence today had been the last loose end in Leo's old life, and he was finally free—when his screwed-up brain allowed him to be. And so he took the phone and called Charlie, and waited with bated breath for him to answer.

'Cause, yeah . . . just the thought of hearing Charlie's voice was still enough to make Leo's heart skip. And damn if Reg's knowing smile didn't say that he saw right through Leo's attempts to play it cool.

It made Leo wonder how he and Charlie had ever kept the fledgling relationship a secret in the first place. Kate and Reg had taken Charlie's coming out with little surprise, and had only seemed mildly more shocked by Leo's. Predictably, their immediate concern had been for the family, and Leo's feet had barely touched the ground before he found himself firmly ensconced in the attic, a laminated sheet with new rules about closed bedroom doors taped to the wall.

Six months down the line and it was funny. At the time? Not so much. And he couldn't deny that despite the skylights above his bed, he missed the comfort of knowing Charlie was just a few feet away. Sleepless nights—of which there were still many—were so much harder when he faced them alone.

"Leo?" Charlie's breathless voice broke into Leo's reverie.

"It's me. Why are you out of breath?"

"I was in the art room. I'm only allowed to answer the phone in reception, remember?"

Leo didn't remember. Part of the curse of his PTSD was apparently that his brain retained every memory that hurt and left no room for the little things that made life special. It wasn't a symptom that Leo had noticed until he'd begun to emerge from the haze of his Darren Stroud–induced meltdown, but it was one he could live with, even if it did mean asking Charlie the same questions a hundred times a day. "How's school?"

"Who cares about school? How was court? Did it go okay?"

Leo glanced at Reg, and then turned away from him slightly, shoving his cap back so he could rest his head on the window. "It was fine. Not as bad as I expected. They asked me a bunch of questions and I answered them."

"What kind of questions?"

"The ones we talked about, you know—the drinking, how long he'd been hitting Mum for, how often he hit me. Some other shit too."

"Like what?"

"If he ever did any weird sexual stuff. I told them he didn't, but I don't know if they believed me."

There was rustling at Charlie's end, and then the sound of a teacher talking sternly, though it didn't seem to be directed at Charlie.

"Why wouldn't they believe you?" Charlie asked after a protracted pause.

Leo shrugged, even though Charlie couldn't see him. "It felt like they wanted me to make it worse than it was. Like what happened wasn't bad enough on its own."

"Did that upset you?"

"No. Damn. You sound like Reg." Beside Leo, Reg chuckled. Leo spared him a glance before he returned his attention to Charlie, who remained silent. "I didn't mean to be dickish."

Charlie sighed. "I know. I just worried about you today. It's not fair that you had to go through it all again. Why couldn't they just use your statement?"

Leo smiled, because despite the heavy content of the conversation, the fierceness with which Charlie often protected him warmed his slowly healing heart. "It had to be done. And now it is."

"Will you know when the trial is over?"

"Yeah. Carol is going to call Reg."

More silence, and Leo knew that Charlie was considering whether Dennis might get off—that he'd be found not guilty and come back to haunt Leo and Lila—but Leo wasn't worried about that. The evidence against Dennis was bulletproof. The bastard was going down, and with any luck, he'd stay down until he was too old to bother anyone but the nurses wiping his arse in a care home.

The negative train of thought took him to the doorway of the dark place his therapist had taught him to avoid. Leo closed his eyes and counted Charlie's breaths, pictured him at home, sitting at the kitchen table with Lila, sketching flowers and ponies, and sighing with mock exasperation when Lila made him colour everything pink. Watching them like that was Leo's happy place—one of them, at least.

How lucky you are to have so many.

Leo opened his eyes. "I'm fine, Charlie. Honest. Please don't worry about me."

"I do try not to. Are you going home now?"

Leo glanced at Reg and repeated the question. Reg nodded. "We just need to stop at B&Q."

"What for?"

"Screws. Then we can finish the goalposts this afternoon."

Leo couldn't hide his glee. While he'd recovered at home—and been suspended from Heyton High—Reg had taken a leave of absence from his teaching job to homeschool Leo so he didn't get behind. For three months, the boring lessons had taken over most mornings, but after lunch, Reg had often taken Leo out to the garage and let him play around with the huge array of tools stored in there, and Leo remained surprised at how much he enjoyed it.

And though he'd been back at school awhile now, the best part was still to come. Their latest project—a set of goalposts for the garden—was nearly finished, and suddenly, Leo couldn't wait to be home. He said good-bye to Charlie and settled back into his seat, unable to contain his excited grin. In return, Reg smiled and turned on Radio Two.

"Kate and I are taking Lila to her first speech therapy session tonight. If we finish the goalposts, perhaps you can convince Charlie to have a kick around in the garden?"

Leo snorted. His own passion for football was slowly returning, but he'd yet to persuade Charlie that it was an activity they could share. "*Give them a ball each,*" he'd said, much to Leo's disgust. "I think he'd rather go to the woods."

"Then do that instead. Either way, get out in the sun. Kate worries about you both being cooped up with the Xbox."

"Kate worries too much."

"I know, but we wouldn't change her, eh?"

Leo could only smile. He'd become closer to Reg than Kate, but he couldn't deny that he loved them both. A new family hadn't been something he'd ever imagined that he'd want. Now?

He couldn't imagine life without them.

Charlie paced Andy and Fliss's small front garden, all the while keeping an ear out for Leo's bike, knowing that he'd come careening down the road with a screech of brakes, like he always did.

It sometimes seemed that Charlie spent every free moment waiting on Leo, but as Leo appeared in the distance, his grin visible and vibrant even from so far away, he wouldn't have had it any other way.

Leo skidded to a halt at Charlie's feet, expertly missing him by mere inches. "Hey."

"Hey yourself. How was football practice?"

"Awesome. I made the team."

"You did? Wow. That's great." Charlie tried not to roll his eyes. Most of the kids on the football team were idiots, but since Leo had returned to school, playing football had done him the world of good, often brightening his mood to the point where his addictive grin was almost constant. "Did Wayne make the team too?"

"Yup. Giving up the fags did the trick. I can hardly catch him now."

"You say that like it's a bad thing." But Charlie said it with a humour that he meant. Wayne had made Leo's return to Heyton High easier in ways that Charlie couldn't, because

Charlie couldn't be everything for Leo, even if he tried. And he certainly didn't want to play football.

"Are you two coming in or what?" Fliss stuck her head out of the open kitchen window. "I promised Mum I'd feed you as soon as you got back. Can't have her precious boys going hungry, can I?"

Charlie treated Fliss to his middle finger, but headed inside anyway. Wednesday night dinners at Fliss's had fast become his favourite time of the week, and it had nothing to do with the food.

Later, after two plates of Fliss's special sausage pie, Charlie and Leo snuck off to the bottom of the huge garden, safe in the knowledge that she wouldn't come looking for them until it was time for her to drive them home. It was the best thing about coming to Fliss's house when Andy was at work, apart from the food . . . that she allowed them a precious few hours of time to themselves, trusting them to be alone, on the condition that they kept their *"bloody shirts on."*

And it was a deal they kept—mostly, because this time really was precious. How could it be anything else when, like now, Leo lay down in the fading sun and gazed up at Charlie like he was the best thing Leo had ever seen?

"Sit down," Leo said impatiently. "I've got something to tell you."

"Something good?"

"Yup."

"Better than making the football team?"

"Yup."

Intrigued, Charlie sat beside Leo, giggling as Leo dragged him down to lie with him. "Stop it. You know Fliss gets all pissy if we come home covered in grass."

"Don't care." Leo tackled Charlie until he had Charlie where he wanted him—beneath him, their legs entangled. He kissed Charlie once . . . twice, before he relented and rolled to one side. "Dennis's verdict was today."

"What?"

"Don't look so shocked. We knew it was coming, right?"

"Um." Charlie opened his mouth. Shut it again. Because it was true that the verdict in Dennis's trial had been due any day for weeks now, but for some reason, he hadn't expected it today. And its arrival didn't meld with the uncharacteristic lightness in Leo's eyes.

Or did it? Charlie sat up abruptly and leaned over Leo, reversing their positions of just a moment ago. "Guilty?"

"Yup. On all counts—murder and attempted murder. Some other shit too."

Other shit. Charlie suppressed a shudder, glad he'd never been fully briefed on all the things Leo's father had inflicted on his family. "Sentence?"

"Not yet, but the judge told him to expect life. Reg says that means at least fifteen years, probably a lot more."

Charlie was still getting used to Leo's ever-growing faith in Reg. It was so far away from the distrust he'd worn like a second skin when he'd shuffled into Charlie's life—and his heart—last winter. "How do you feel about it? Happy?"

"Would you think me a monster if I said yes?"

"No. Your dad is a bastard."

"He's not my dad, Charlie. Wasn't long before he killed Mum."

Mum. It was the first time Leo had ever referred to his mother like that in front of Charlie. On the rare occasions he'd mentioned her, it had always been *my mum* or *Wendy*. Charlie wanted to stop a moment and consider what that meant, but with the shadows still absent from Leo's clear gaze, he let it go. And with that release came an epiphany: the light in Leo was that of freedom. Justice had been served, and Leo and Lila could finally move on.

Charlie fiddled with the frayed edges of the bandage around Leo's elbow. It was much smaller than the one Leo had arrived with so long ago, even with the minor surgery he'd endured a few weeks ago to repair the failed skin graft, and its shrinking size was yet another reminder of how far Leo had come in the last few months.

Leo sat up, mirroring Charlie's pose, and gently reclaimed his arm, the wooden beads around his wrist rattling with the movement. "You seem different."

"Different? Since when?"

Leo shrugged. "I don't know."

"That doesn't make any sense."

"What does?"

Leo had Charlie there. "Maybe it's my hair. I had it cut after school."

"Yeah, I noticed that. It's shorter at the sides and longer on top. Like the dudes you've been drawing, right?"

Leo had little interest in art, but he seemed to like watching Charlie draw, like the stroke of the pens on the paper soothed him somehow. "Yes, it's kind of manga style, but not as big. I've wanted it like this for ages, but—" Charlie broke off and fingered his hair that now rivalled Leo's in length, though it was nothing like Leo's wild curls. "I thought people would laugh at me, but I don't care anymore."

"I didn't know you ever did."

Charlie shrugged. "Neither did I really, but I suppose I must have done."

"Now you're not making sense."

"Sorry."

"Nah, Charlie . . . don't be sorry. Not with me." Leo was suddenly in Charlie's face, his forehead finding its groove in

Charlie's, like they'd been made to be pressed together this way. "I wouldn't be here without you. You know that, don't you?"

Charlie gulped at the lump in his throat. He didn't like to think about the rough months they'd lived through before Leo's undiagnosed PTSD had finally broken him down. Leo's crying in the night. The emptiness in his eyes. "What did I do?"

"You reminded me to be happy."

"Are you happy, Leo?"

"I'm learning."

It was a phrase Charlie had heard a lot recently, but it had never sounded as good as it did right now. Charlie grinned so hard his face hurt, and he lunged at Leo, but before their lips met in a kiss that Charlie needed as much as air, Fliss's voice reached them, summoning them inside.

They both knew better than to ignore her. It was only last week that she'd turned the hose on them. With rueful groans, they hauled themselves up from the grass and jogged up the long garden.

Fliss waited for them at the back door. At first nothing seemed amiss, and then Charlie saw him—the tall, dark-haired man who hovered behind her. Charlie slowed to a stop, apprehension creeping into the persistent happy bubble in his belly. He'd heard rumours of Fliss having a new boyfriend, and had even expected to meet him sometime soon, but the unease in his gut wasn't for him. Leo's reactions to new people—new *men*— were still unpredictable.

The obvious caution in Fliss's face didn't help. Her smile was forced as she stepped outside and beckoned the tall dude to follow. "This is Steve," she said. "Steve, these two goons are my brothers."

She stared hard at Charlie, clearly hoping that he could act normally enough to make up for whatever Leo was doing behind him. But as he opened his mouth to grind out a mechanical greeting, Leo breezed past him, stepping in front of him and extending his hand.

"Hi, Steve. I'm Leo."

Charlie blinked, and the surprise in Fliss's face mirrored his own, but as Leo glanced over his shoulder and spared him a playful wink, he mouthed three little words that meant the whole world.

I am Leo.

Charlie smiled and lifted his hand to sign back, "Yes, *you are.*"

NEWSLETTER

For the most up to date news and free books, subscribe to my newsletter HERE.

This is a zero spam zone. Maximum number of emails you will receive is one per month.

PATREON

Not ready to let go of Charlie and Leo? Or looking for sneak peeks at future books in the series? Alternative POVs, outtakes, and missing moments from **all** Garrett's books can be found on her Patreon site. Misfits, Slide, Strays...the works. Because you know what? Garrett wasn't ready to let her boys go either.

Pledges start from as little as $2, and all content is available at the lowest tier.

ACKNOWLEDGMENTS

Thanks as always to my wonderful editors, Caz and Alex, and to the sensitivity readers who helped so much with the BSL. Also to Jem Roche, who offered insight to the English foster care system very early on in the writing of *Finding Home*.

I wrote this book for my daughter, Darcey. Darlin', if you made it to the end, I love you, and am more proud of you than I could ever say. Now tidy your bloody room.

ABOUT GARRETT LEIGH

Bonus Material available for all books on Garrett's Patreon account. Includes short stories from Misfits, Slide, Strays, What Remains, Dream, and much more. Sign up here: https://www.patreon.com/garrettleigh

Facebook Fan Group, Garrett's Den... https://www.facebook.com/groups/garre...

Garrett Leigh is an award-winning British writer, cover artist, and book designer. Her debut novel, Slide, won Best Bisexual Debut at the 2014 Rainbow Book Awards, and her polyamorous novel, Misfits was a finalist in the 2016 LAMBDA awards, and was again a finalist in 2017 with Rented Heart.

In 2017, she won the EPIC award in contemporary romance with her military novel, Between Ghosts, and the contemporary romance category in the Bisexual Book Awards with her novel What Remains.

When not writing, Garrett can generally be found procrastinating on Twitter, cooking up a storm, or sitting on her behind doing as little as possible, all the while shouting at her menagerie of children and animals and attempting to tame her unruly and wonderful FOX.

Garrett is also an award winning cover artist, taking the silver medal at the Benjamin Franklin Book Awards in 2016. She designs for various publishing houses and independent authors at blackjazzdesign.com, and co-owns the specialist stock site moonstockphotography.com

Connect with Garrett
www.garrettleigh.com

Only Love

Heart

What Remains

What Matters

Between Ghosts